PACIFIC PASSAGES

By

Mark A. Putch

© 2002 by Mark A. Putch. All rights reserved.

No part of this book may be reproduced, stored in a retrieval system, or transmitted by any means, electronic, mechanical, photocopying, recording, or otherwise, without written permission from the author.

ISBN: 1-4033-1461-6

This book is printed on acid free paper.

1stBooks - rev. 06/05/02

DISCLAIMER

Pacific Passages is a work of fiction. Names, characters, places and incidents either are the product of the author's imagination or are used fictitiously, and any resemblance to actual persons, living or dead, business establishments, events or locales is entirely coincidental.

DEDICATION

To Candy, Amy and Stacey

ACKNOWLEDGEMENTS

Greatest appreciation to Henri Forget, editor, and many thanks to members of Prose on the Plains critique group: Sonja Craig, Kay Galvan, Elaine Heise, Candy Putch, Laurie Wasmund and Mary Welty.

PACIFIC PASSAGES

On a summer Sunday afternoon, Janelle busied herself in the kitchen putting the finishing touches on lunch. Out back, I stood over a hot grill, wincing in the smoke, rotating planks of swordfish and sniffing the aroma of mesquite. The heat from the grill and the sun drew sweat from my sunburned face.

My eyes welled up in tears, but what caused me to weep was the feeling of loss, and not the wisps of smoke that wrapped around me. I dried my eyes with my shirtsleeves and stared at the fresh-cut grass, which suddenly seemed futile and irrelevant.

Kurt and his girlfriend, Bridget, were coming over for a patio picnic.

Janelle slid the patio door open, poked her head through and said, "Honey, they're pulling up the driveway."

"Get them a drink and send 'em back."

"Sure you want to open the wine from pilot training?" she asked, looking confused.

"Yes, we need to drink it today," I said, as if it were about to expire; the wine was only twenty-five years old. I knew it would be our last opportunity, but I couldn't tell Janelle that. "Bring it out with lunch though. Give them something else for now."

"Okay, how much longer?"

"Ten minutes max."

"Here." Janelle handed me the tableware before sliding the door shut, pushing a gust of cold air my way.

In the cover of shade, I was setting the table when Kurt walked out. It never failed to amaze me to watch him walk without the slightest hint of a limp since the accident.

"Hi Kurt, welcome."

He seemed on edge; both hands held beers.

As I lifted the hood of the grill, white smoke swelled off the hot grates and sizzling steaks of fish.

"Smells good," Kurt said.

"What have you been up to today?"

Kurt looked around and whispered, "Fixed a bug in the program this morning. It works perfect." He took a long pull from the can of beer.

"That's a relief."

"Bridget's ready, too."

"Good." My eyes were focused on the sliding door. "Is Bridget handling the stress okay?"

"Here, here," Kurt said holding his beer up. "Speaking of the devil."

"Duff, that smell is wonderful," she said walking out with a glass of Chardonnay.

"Thanks. How are you, Bridget?" I gave her a hug. She felt tense. I liked Bridget. She was good for Kurt.

Kurt took a seat. "Do you care where we eat?"

"No, sit anywhere. The kids are going to eat on the picnic bench." I pointed to it under the eucalyptus tree. I stuck a fork in the fish. "Just a couple more minutes."

"Yard looks good," Kurt said.

"It's coming along." I had put in new rock and bushes in the flowerbeds and planted two cherry trees since the beginning of summer, the last time Kurt and Bridget were visiting.

"Wish I could get Kurt into yard work."

"The rocks are nice," Kurt said and drank from his second beer, peering out from behind dark sunglasses. "I know good yard work when I see it."

Janelle poked her head out the sliding door. "I need help with the food, Duff."

"Start with the appetizers." I made several trips bringing out the food and the cherished bottle of wine. I put a large piece of fish on each plate. Tender white meat, seared with swaths of black, basted with the succulent sauce that was Janelle's secret recipe. I wanted that recipe.

We sat at the table while Janelle went to the front yard to get the kids. I whispered to them, "Last chance to back out. Is it a go?"

"Yes," Bridget whispered while gazing at the patio door.

Kurt gave a thumbs-up sign. "It's a go," he hissed from stiff lips.

"Talked to Marcia this morning. She's in."

Kurt and Bridget nodded.

We connected hands briefly as if we were going to pray.

"Act as if everything is okay between me and Janelle. She knows you know about the divorce, but she'll be more relaxed if it feels just like old times. We can't afford to raise any suspicions in her mind, especially now. There's not enough time to put out any more fires."

Both nodded, but frankly I was worried about Kurt because he had been drinking hard. When he gets drunk, he says things. Obviously the stress was mounting on him.

Janelle gave the kids their food. The boys were six and eight; their father lived in L.A.

Janelle touched me on the shoulder as she sat down.

"Let's eat," I said.

"Everything looks good," Bridget said.

I poured the wine, explaining that it was the last bottle I'd saved from pilot training graduation twenty-five years earlier. Placing the wineglasses before each of us, I said, "A toast."

We lifted the glasses.

"To wonderful friends, the end of another beautiful summer, the annual Labor Day barbecue, and lastly, to the future."

"Cheers," the three said in unison, then drank.

"That's a lot to toast," Kurt said. "We'd better toast each one individually."

We drank to several toasts. Over the course of lunch it became a contest to offer a toast more clever than the previous one. We had a grand time, drinking that bottle and several bottles of less distinguished wines. We all got drunk that afternoon. Even Janelle loosened up a bit.

At one point, Janelle emptied a bottle of wine into our glasses. "I propose a toast," she said and smiled at me with her glass lifted.

I lifted my glass and nodded.

"To great friends."

"Cheers," I said, clinking glasses with her. I knew what she meant.

Kurt and Bridget echoed the cheers.

Janelle pecked me on the cheek as she went inside to get another bottle of wine.

"Thanks, honey." I felt sad that things hadn't worked out between us.

After lunch, we talked. Fresh and interesting topics diverted out attentions from the mounting pressure that permeated our every thought. We discussed the subjects as if we might never broach them again. It was a sort of final treatise, so everybody was very specific and intense.

The tension was near the surface, but our collective intellects—assisting each other—staved off its growing presence.

All was well until Janelle started talking about the airline, a not-so-fresh topic.

She said, "I read that McClusky is selling off the Pacific."

"The board approved it last week," Kurt said.

"How does Pacifica benefit?" she asked.

"They don't, do they?" Bridget said looking at me.

"Hell no. We lose all the way around. The Pacific routes are the most profitable routes we fly."

"We won't make it through the winter without the Pacific," Kurt said.

"Then why would he sell it?" Janelle asked.

"Greed," Kurt said. "The bastard."

"Eighty-seven million is what I read in the *Wall Street Journal*," Bridget said.

"McClusky gets eighty-seven million. Another hundred and twenty million goes to his cronies," I said.

Janelle wore a frown. "What happens to the employees?"

"They get screwed," Bridget said.

"Or, we get to start over—again. With Air Tasmania this time," Kurt said, taking a gulp of wine.

"By the way," Bridget looked at Janelle, "McClusky was on the board of directors at Air Tasmania not too long ago."

"No," Janelle said.

"Yes!" Kurt said, plunking his empty wineglass on the table.

To get off the subject, I said, looking toward the boys, "Why don't we play badminton?"

"Yeah," the boys said.

We played several sets. The vigorousness with which we played the game proved to be another good diversion.

Janelle dropped the thorny airline subject; the party went smoothly from there.

We walked Kurt and Bridget to their car about five o'clock, much earlier than usual, but Kurt and Bridget were ready to go. The three of us had no reason to prolong things for fear of slipping up, and everybody was exhausted anyway.

Kurt and Bridget hugged Janelle. Everything seemed just as it had been before.

Bridget started the car. "Thanks again," she said.

"Enjoyed it," Kurt said, buckling his seatbelt.

"See you Tuesday, Kurt," I said, staring into his eyes.

"See ya then." He turned away.

I couldn't help feeling anxious, transferring my own doubt, wondering if Kurt was up to it, but I knew better. Anticipation—not the battle itself—was the worst cause of fear.

"Good night."

They backed out of the driveway.

****

Tuesday morning came early, what with last-minute preparations. I couldn't sleep despite a critical need for it. How could anyone sleep anyway? There were a million things left to do, and I wanted them all done at once.

At six a.m. I departed from home, looking in on Janelle one last time while she slept. Our relationship was over, I thought, imagining her in her lover's arms by noon. She still didn't know that I knew, but I had hired a private investigator when she filed for divorce three months ago.

My strategy was to reveal my information when she hit me up again, as she threatened, going all the way, as she put it, for the juicy settlement. I thought about the boys but couldn't bring myself to see them. They were good kids.

I placed an oversized suitcase in the Audi and drove toward San Francisco. With so many things to do, my mind raced at Mach speed. Although stressed, I knew how to handle it.

I'd learned in the Army to concentrate on one well-planned task at a time, each neatly compartmentalized. Accomplishing multiple tasks under a time limit is procedural and procedure becomes the all-consuming issue, much like flying in combat.

You don't have time to worry about getting shot down in combat because there's too much to do. If you do get shot down, well, that involves another procedure. You don't start worrying—really worrying—until you found yourself hiding in the jungle from shit-smelling soldiers ferreting around and whispering to each other in a language you don't know. Then you're scared—real scared.

Completing the *well-structured tasks*, I showed up at Operations an hour earlier than normal. It was three p.m., the designated time I was to meet my first officer, Lee Maddox. I needed to brief him on some areas that we didn't get to talk about on the previous trip.

Lee was a new-hire pilot with Pacifica and I was his line instructor. Lee was married to one of our female pilots and had been a flight attendant with Pacifica for five years. Then he took a three-year piloting job with a commuter airline to gain experience before Pacifica would hire him as a pilot. Lee still lacked significant experience and was not exactly an ace but had a great attitude and was competent and safe. Lee needed more instruction, I decided on the last trip, before I could sign him off.

We met in the briefing room. Concentrating very hard on what I said to him kept my mind off everything else. We talked about the nuances of flying the Boeing 727.

Looking at my watch, I said to him, "Second officer will be here in a few minutes. Do you know Kurt Lamar?"

"I know who he is."

"He's our engineer today."

"Didn't he have an accident or something?"

"Yeah, about ten years ago. He was the national aerobatics champion when he crashed a Pitts. Lost a foot."

"You'd never know it."

"He's got a prosthetic foot from just above the left ankle."

"How'd it happen?"

"Trying to outrun a thunderstorm in Topeka. Didn't have enough gas to go anywhere else. He ground looped it in the gust front. They pulled him from the fire in the pouring rain."

"Ouch! Is that why he's still an engineer?" Lee studied the paper with the crew names and their seniority numbers.

"Yeah."

"Isn't the FAA loosening up on letting guys fly with handicaps?"

"They are. If Kurt shows the FAA he can handle an airliner with an engine out, they'd give him his medical back." I couldn't tell Lee that despite advancements in prosthesis, what science would never give back to Kurt was the confidence he needed to fly an airplane.

"Is he trying to get it back?"

"I think so," I lied to him. Kurt would never fly again. The idea of just touching the controls frightens him to death. This I'd known because he told me over and over again.

"Looks like Kurt's senior to you. He could be a captain."

"Yes, he is, and he *could* be a captain." Becoming irritated with Lee's persistence, I changed the tack. "Kurt and I flew together at Coastal."

"I had some friends at Coastal," Lee said.

"Kurt came here as soon as the bankruptcy was announced. I hung on to the end. I was a senior captain with more to lose."

"Kurt made a wise choice."

"He did. It took me two more years to see what he saw. That's why he's two years senior to me."

"Smart man, Kurt is."

I explained to Lee that Kurt had been an intern for Coastal and hired at the age of twenty-three.

"The intern program is hard to get into at Pacifica. I know, I tried," Lee said.

"It was tough at Coastal, too."

"What did you fly at Coastal?"

"Seven-twenty-seven. Same as here. I'm an old die-hard."

"Was Kurt a captain?"

"First officer."

Lee nodded.

"Things change fast in the airlines. Kurt was my first officer at Coastal but I was his first officer at Pacifica—before the accident."

"What happened to Coastal?"

"Lots, but essentially deregulation did 'em in." I looked at my watch. "Flight plans should be up now."

We met Kurt in the flight planning room of Operations at four p.m. We studied the data—weather, weights, fuel, logbook, route of flight, etc. I signed a release for all three legs we were scheduled to fly. We had a five o'clock pushback for Phoenix with a return flight to San Francisco, then on to a nice layover in Vancouver, B.C.

My plan was to cut Lee loose after the Phoenix turn if everything went well.

We added five thousand pounds of fuel on the Phoenix-to-San Francisco leg because San Francisco got backlogged so easily, I explained to Lee, who nodded agreeably.

I sent Kurt and Lee ahead while I checked my mailbox for flight manual revisions.

"We'll see you at the jet." Kurt gave me a skulking glance and nod, confirming his readiness.

"Take Lee with you on the walk-around, so he can get an idea of what goes on out there," I said.

"Okay."

The flight to Phoenix went smoothly. On climb-out, I noted a thick hovering fog extending from the Golden Gate to Monterey Bay. I worried that the return flight could be delayed if the fog moved inland.

Phoenix was typically hot: one hundred degrees at six o'clock in the evening. Lee made a fine landing despite desert thermals pitching us up and down through the frenzied air. Watching him closely throughout the flight, I decided he was ready.

We parked the jet, thanked the passengers, and went to eat Mexican food. The restaurant was where the local Mexicans went. Carlos, the station manager and old friend, had told me about the place many years ago.

I first met Carlos twenty-five years ago when I was going through Air Force pilot training at Williams AFB, near Phoenix. Carlos had been a flight-line supervisor back then. Carlos lent us his car, as he always did. We were back in an hour.

"Thanks, Carlos," I said handing him his keys. "Delicious as usual."

"You're always welcome to it. I tell my brother-in-law you liked it."

We talked about old times, then he said, "Got a good load tonight," pointing outside to an armored courier truck with armed guards standing around it.

"Good. How much?"

"Thirty-eight million, four hundred thousand." Carlos smiled, showing the gold tooth with the star in it.

"I was hoping for more," I joked.

"Too heavy this time of year. Every seat's taken. You're up to the max."

"Yeah?"

"The money's in twenty-dollar bills. Weighs over 4000 pounds itself."

"I see," I said. "How many boxes?"

Mark A. Putch

"About two hundred. My guys are complaining already."

I laughed.

We finished the paperwork, and I confirmed the extra 5000 pounds of fuel with the fueler.

"Any flow control into San Francisco?" I asked, thinking about the fog.

Carlos rummaged through a stack of computer messages. "I don't see anything. Looks good."

"Good. We'll see you later, Carlos. Thanks for everything."

"Okay, Duff. Have a good flight."

We shook hands firmly and held the grip for several seconds.

I went up to the flight deck. Kurt was outside doing the walk-around, and I sent Lee to the gate podium for the weight manifest. Four flight attendants boarded the airplane. Marcia, the first flight attendant, boarded last, coming in the cockpit.

"We're here, captain."

I got out of my seat, saying, "You look fabulous. I love that perfume." I pressed hard against her, backing her into the bulkhead. I burned with passion as I kissed her.

"I love you," she said.

"I want to ravish you."

"Control yourself. We've got too much work to do," Marcia said.

"Right." I shifted gears like a schizophrenic. "How was the layover?"

"Fine. How's everything else?"

"It's a go. Right on schedule. They're loading the money."

"Good, I'm ready. I want him in first class. I changed my mind. It works better that way."

"Okay. That's what I thought all along." I began to think. "First class is full."

"I told the agent that 4A is blocked off," she said. "If he doesn't bite, I'll work it from the front."

"Right, best place for him. I know all about this guy, though. He's such a lush. Probably drunk already. It'll be easy," I reassured her.

"I'll upgrade him as soon as the door's closed. I'll call you when it's done."

"Beautiful." I saw Lee approaching on the Jetway. "Cool it, here comes Lee." I nodded.

"Okay." She looked straight at me. "I can't wait to get there," she whispered.

Lee entered the cockpit.

PACIFIC PASSAGES

"Lee, I want you to meet Marcia. She's our first flight attendant today." They looked closely at one another as if they might know each other. "Lee was a Pacifica flight attendant once upon a time."

"Congratulations. I like to see the company grow from within. Nice to meet you, Lee." She shook his hand.

"My pleasure."

Marcia busied herself with cabin preflight duties while the cockpit crew prepared for the flight. I mapped out the route and set up the radios. Kurt worked on the weight manifest and Lee got the clearance from Air Traffic Control. The agent came down asking Marcia if she was ready for the passengers. She said yes.

The first passenger was Cluny Taggart, who introduced himself to the cockpit.

"Captain, I'm Cluny Taggart, your courier." He handed me a form designating his position with Aegis Security Corporation and gave me a packet of contingency procedures with his courier identification badge clipped to it. I studied the photo of a younger, leaner Cluny before his chin swelled over his starched bureaucratic collar.

I handed the ID to him saying, "Looks like you, Cluny." I shook his padded hand, his grip listless. I got a good look at his ruddy face with its dark stubble bristling from the hollows of a pockmarked surface. He met my expectations. His shaved head was round as a basketball, a complement to bloodshot eyes set in deep sockets, shadowed by a hairless brow. He wore a polyester suit with black athletic shoes and carried a tattered vinyl briefcase.

He smiled without elan.

"You armed, Cluny?"

"No."

"No?" I said with surprise, to verify.

"Nope, not armed."

"Marcia," I said, projecting my voice toward the cabin door. "Come in, please."

She looked at me as she entered the cockpit. "Yes, captain?"

"Marcia, this is Mr. Cluny Taggart, the courier. We're moving a large sum of money to San Francisco, and Mr. Taggart is responsible for it. Would you show him to his seat?"

"Sure." She shook his hand with an attractive smile on her face. "Nice to meet you, Mr. Taggart. Follow me, please."

Cluny trailed obediently in what seemed slow motion.

We finished the preflight, summarized by a reading of the checklist while the passengers boarded. Some of them stuck their heads through the cockpit door on the way to their seats. We treated them cordially, striking up small talk about the flight.

Some kids came up with their parents and we took photos of them sitting in the captain's seat wearing my hat. "Stop by on the way out in San Francisco if you have any questions," I said out of habit. They were excited about flying.

"Duff," Kurt said urgently.

"What's up?"

"Carlos wants to talk to you on the radio."

I turned the volume up on Kurt's radio, keyed the microphone, and said, "Phoenix Operations, Pacifica 1497, go ahead."

"Duff, Carlos here."

"Go Carlos."

"Just got a call from Seattle. They want you to take a ten-minute delay for a human heart en route to the airport. A guy in San Francisco needs it bad. Says he's in emergency surgery right now. Are you agreeable?"

My mind went blank. "Did you hear that, Kurt?"

"Yes." His eyes widened and shoulders shrugged.

Everything was already so tight, but how could I leave without the life-saving heart? "Yes, we'll delay. "Can we can get it quicker?"

"Stand by."

Three minutes later Carlos keyed, "Duff, Carlos again."

"Go."

"It's on the airfield. Should have it on board in four or five minutes."

"Good. Have the agent close the door and give us the paperwork through my window."

"No problem. We'll push you off the gate so you can start engines while we load it," Carlos said.

"Very well. You run a hell of a station, Carlos."

"Tell my boss that. I need a raise."

"Count on it."

"Okay Duff, have a good flight."

"Pacifica 1497 out."

The agent slammed the door after saying, "Have a good one, guys."

"Thanks, mate. You, too," I said.

Kurt and Lee were starting engines one and two when the cabin chimes rang three minutes after pushback.

"Engine room," I said, answering the phone.

"He's in 4A. All it took was the grace of the captain's complimentary first-class upgrade and of course a bottle of our best house wine," Marcia reported wryly.

"Nice touch. Keep me posted."

She elaborated by saying, "Piece of cake."

I knew Marcia would have no problem with Cluny, who probably hadn't had a beautiful woman pay attention to him in a long time.

Carlos zipped toward the airplane driving a tug. The heart was in a red cooler with HUMAN ORGAN written across it. He handed it to a baggage loader who cautiously secured it in the forward cargo hold. I waved at Carlos. He gave us a thumbs-up sign and a wave-off salute.

"Turn number three," I commanded. To save time I called ground control for taxi instructions while they started the third motor. Designating the flight as being critical to human life, I prefaced the call sign with "Lifeguard," which assured priority handling with air-traffic control.

Ground sent us to runway 25 Right with instructions to cross it halfway down and taxi to the end on a parallel taxiway. This placed us number one for takeoff on the south side of the runway ahead of a long lineup of aircraft closely queued on the north side.

We lifted off five minutes late. I was confident of making up the time.

I looked at Lee. "Let's do eight-four at twenty-six," meaning our cruise speed would be Mach .84, or eighty-four percent of the speed of sound, at twenty-six thousand feet. I explained to him that at a lower altitude we'd get a higher true airspeed, with a better chance of making up the five minutes. He already knew that but remained the obedient and receptive student.

"Yes, sir," he said. "Kurt, would you give me numbers for eight-four, please?"

"Sure, have them right up," Kurt said.

Lee knew I was evaluating how he got along with the crew. He had good people skills. I think it was his experience as a flight attendant that helped him.

Reaching cruise altitude, I studied the route closely. From Las Vegas we were filed along a narrow corridor to the northwest, along the Nevada-California line. The flight path straddled the gunnery ranges of Nellis Air Force Base to the east, and the Fort Irwin Complex to the west. I knew a major military exercise was taking place there. Restricted to the west of Tonopah, our arrival fix for San Francisco was Coaldale, Nevada.

"Should we ask for direct?" Lee asked.

"No, the ranges are hot. They won't give it to us tonight," I said.

"Just thinking of ways to save time," Lee said.

"Good thought. You're on the right track." Having never flown in the military, Lee wasn't expected to know about the ranges, although many pilots would have thought he should know. "You're doing fine."

Lee smiled and nodded.

The cabin chimes rang again.

Kurt picked it up. "Kurt here. Yes, I'll tell him." He tapped me on the shoulder.

I had just been given a new radio frequency from Los Angeles Air-Traffic Control Center. I stood my right index finger up for delay as I dialed in the numbers because I didn't want to forget the frequency. I checked in with Oakland Center.

Looking back to Kurt, I said, "Go ahead."

"Marcia needs you in the back when you get a chance."

I nodded to him while touching Lee on the arm. "I'm going to step back for a few minutes."

"Okay."

"I'll get the radios for you," Kurt said.

"Thanks," Lee said as he pulled the oxygen mask down and donned it, giving me a thumbs-up when he was ready.

I walked into the cabin glancing at 4A but not seeing anyone sitting there. I met Marcia in the galley. She was standing in the far corner, away from the passengers. She pulled me close nuzzling her face against mine. I wrapped my arms around her thin waist and clutched close to her curves. She smelled great—like the cosmetic section of Neiman Marcus.

"How's everything?" I asked, arching back to get a good look into her eyes.

"He's gone."

"Outstanding. How'd you do it?"

"Easy. I gave him the bottle of wine and told him it was from you. He was flattered but said he wasn't allowed to drink on duty but that he could use a Coke. I put it in the Coke and he drank it like a schoolboy drinking his mother's medicine. He was so cute when his eyes rolled back," she said sardonically.

"And he's out?"

"He'll be asleep until this time tomorrow," she promised, backed by the shimmer of sky-blue eyes and the flutter of eyelashes.

"You're so cute when you're devious. A diva of deceit, a bounteous beauty, you are." I kissed her.

"There's a compliment somewhere in that." She put her arms on my shoulders, pulling me close. "Kiss me again."

I kissed her passionately, massaging her shoulders and back with rippling strokes.

She squeezed the sides of my face with her palms.

My cheeks felt hot, like fiery eruptions of clay. I cut the groping short. "Is that complimentary enough?"

"No. More."

"Later."

I smiled at her, pulling back again, my hands slipping off her sharp hips.

"How much longer?" she asked.

"Twenty-five minutes. It's a go."

"I'm ready."

"I almost forgot. Let him keep the wine." I grinned.

Marcia smiled, covering her mouth. "I put it in the seat next to him. It'll be waiting when he wakes up."

"He'll need it."

Marcia smiled and nodded as she lightly tapped my shoulder.

I went back to the cockpit. Lee took off the mask. "Everything's fine," I said.

Lee smiled.

I studied the maps closely, helping Lee navigate. Kurt stared at his map, which he had laid out on the flight engineer's desk. Lee handled the airplane pretty well. He stayed ahead of it and was relatively smooth. I stayed abreast of our exact position over the warm, opaque Nevada desert floor, awash in the brightness of a waning full moon.

I waited patiently, like a flight simulator instructor waiting for the programmed malfunction to occur. In a sinister sort of way, having been a longtime observer of human factors, I was always amazed to watch crews scurry around—often panicked—trying to handle fabricated emergencies. I had been an instructor for many years, teaching new pilots in simulators. My mind was clear, as it had been in simulators; the wheels turned and the emotional and intellectual barriers to passing over the edge vanished.

Kurt said calmly, "Duff, I've got three icing lights on back here."

I jerked my head back toward his panel to see the three illuminated amber lights, verifying Kurt's assertion.

Lee flinched, his face contorted.

"Lee, I'm going to pull the power back very slowly. We may have fuel contamination. You're still flying," I said.

"Okay." Lee looked scared.

I popped the speed brake out. "We need to slow down." I looked at Lee. "You still have it. Slow to three hundred knots."

When the speed brake opened, an emergency locator transmitter with a thirty-minute delay deployed from the airplane, parachuting to an isolated position on the Nevada desert, providing a fabricated crash site and thirty minutes to work with. Kurt pulled the transponder circuit breaker so that air-traffic control would lose our radar return.

"Okay. I'm still flying." His voice quivered.

"I'm going to go through the checklist with Kurt."

"Do you want me to declare an emergency with center?" Lee asked.

"Not yet."

The checklist recommended an immediate landing because of the possibility of fuel starvation to all three engines. I instructed Kurt to keep his eyes on the engine instruments, particularly the fuel-flow indicators.

"Should we contact the company?" Lee asked.

"Not yet. Just keep her steady and on course until I figure this out."

"Pacifica 1497, we've lost your transponder. Squawk 3565," Oakland Center said over the radio.

"Roger, Oakland. Squawking 3565, Lifeguard Pacifica 1497," I said keying the radio. I set 3565 in the transponder window.

Kurt leaned forward, speaking loudly. "We need to land now. We're going to lose power."

"Lifeguard Pacifica 1497, negative squawk. Radar contact lost," Oakland said, his voice an octave higher.

"Stand by Oakland, Pacific 1497. I'll check it and call you back," I said. "Kurt, check the transponder's circuit breaker."

"Roger."

We were in position. The airport was twenty-five miles away and we were at 26,000 feet. "We've got to land there," I said firmly, pointing short of the lights of Tonopah.

"I don't see the airport," Lee said.

"I'll talk you through it. Start a steep descent. We're too high."

"Are you sure, Duff? Shouldn't we let the company know?" he asked with a confused look.

"That's not important. Not enough time. We've got to get this airplane on the ground before the engines flame out, or else we'll all die," I said with my best captain's authority.

Lee didn't respond.

"Lee, I'm pulling the speed brake out to help us get down. Put the nose down about ten degrees." I cautiously pulled the throttles back to idle.

Lee responded to my commands but remained silent.

"Kurt, let Marcia know what's happening. Have her brief the passengers. Be on the ground in…seven minutes."

"Right," Kurt said as he picked up the telephone, ringing the chimes.

"Marcia, Kurt here. We're making an emergency landing. Fuel contamination. Yes, that's right. Make quick prep. Seven minutes tops." He hung up.

The airport was forty miles from Tonopah. The runway lay in a desolate valley between two north-south running mountain ranges. I had discovered the nameless airstrip while flying for the Army and landed there again years later as a reservist on deployments to Red Flag and Air Warrior. It was an uncontrolled, auxiliary airfield built during World War II. Nobody used it except an occasional military pilot out exploring the countryside. The airport didn't have fuel or services, but nobody else needed to know that. The 8000-foot runway was paved but dark. It had no runway lights.

"Lee, I'm going to talk you down. I think you can handle it." I turned down the volume of the radios, silencing the incessant chatter of Oakland Center.

"Shouldn't we be talking to center?" he asked.

We were dropping out of the sky real fast, like a dive-bomber. "Too low now. Can't get them." The mountain peaks rose up toward us. "All that matters now is to get this jet on the ground. Oakland can't help us do that."

"We'll call them on the ground," Kurt said, cutting the tension.

Lee capitulated. "I'm not sure about this, but you're the captain."

"Turn thirty degrees right. I've got the power at idle for you." The airspeed accelerated toward 400 knots.

Lee said nothing but did as I told him. His breathing was loud and erratic.

"Shallow the descent and slow to 270."

"Okay," he mumbled.

"Kurt, give us a card for max landing weight."

"Got it ready." He handed it to me.

"Pull the nose up a little more. Hold it there. Good. Set your speeds. I'll read them off for you."

"I can hardly breathe," Lee said as he set the reference speeds on his airspeed indicator with a trembling hand.

"Relax, man. We're going to make it," I said.

"You can do it, Lee," Kurt said.

Taking the controls, I said, "I've got it. Take a couple deep breaths and loosen up."

"Sorry, I'm just scared," Lee said.

"We're all scared."

"You can do it," Kurt repeated louder.

"You've got it back."

Lee took the controls. "Okay, I've got it."

I put the gear down. "Don't level off. Continue the descent. The speed brake's still out. We're going to come down like a rock."

"I still don't see the runway," Lee said, quite concerned.

"We're on course. You'll see it in a minute. Keep her coming. Increase the descent."

"Okay."

Whoop, Whoop! "Pull up!" *Whoop, Whoop!* "Pull up!" the aircraft warning system barked, a flashing red light illuminating the cockpit.

"Not that much. Pull back on the yoke." I added pressure to the yoke, helping him level off. The warning ceased.

"Got too close to that ridge over there," Kurt said, pointing out my side window.

"Shit," Lee said.

"Turn another twenty degrees right," I said. "Keep the airplane over the valley."

Lee hesitated.

"You're still flying, Lee."

"Sorry," Lee said. "Twenty right."

"Before-landing checklist," I said, directing my voice at Kurt.

"Roger." Kurt read it aloud as I responded to it.

"I still don't see the runway. You should fly it." Lee looked panicked when he glanced at me.

"No, you're doing fine. Five right. Don't worry about the 250 below ten," I said, meaning the FAA speed restriction of 250 knots below 10,000 feet. "Keep her coming down—it's okay—we're over the valley now."

"Huh? Shouldn't we be going toward those lights?" Lee pointed to the glow of lights on the horizon.

"Damn, we can't make Tonopah now. We're too low. We've got to land now," I shouted, the lights disappearing behind the mountain ridge. "Keep her coming down."

Lee turned his head to the flight instruments, staring in silence. He seemed to lose all situational awareness then. The instruments acted like magnets, sucking his energies into the black hole of tunnel vision. The ex-flight attendant—severely limited in experience—was task saturated. I'd seen it before.

Passing through 8000 feet at 270 knots, descending fast at 6000 feet per minute, the ground rushed up at us. We were just a few thousand feet above the valley floor.

A cockpit spotlight shone on Lee's glistening face: tendons flexed at the jaw, neck muscles pulled taut, and eyes channeled into darkness. His brow bled beads of sweat.

"Lee, snap out of it," I shouted.

"Oh, yeah. Sorry."

The runway lay just ten miles ahead: time to slow down and get the landing flaps out. "Level off and slow down. Pull the nose up a little more." I remained calm but ready to take over if Lee lost it again.

"Kurt, put the flaps out on schedule." Lee kept me too busy to worry about the flaps.

"Okay. Two degrees," he announced placing the lever at the two-degree detent as the speed decreased to below the speed for the flaps at that setting.

A loud *Beep, Beep, Beep...* sounded from the airplane as the flaps began to extend.

Lee jerked his head, looking around the cockpit.

"It's the speed brake," Kurt said.

I nodded.

Lee turned back to the instruments.

I let the horn beep until we were below 200 knots, then retracted the speed brake. The horn silenced.

Kurt worked the flaps precisely, announcing his actions: "Five degrees, fifteen degrees, twenty degrees, twenty-five degrees," and, finally, "thirty degrees," as the airspeed bled off. The airplane approached a normal glidepath.

"Another five right. You see the runway out there about seven miles ahead?" I said.

"No," Lee shouted.

"I see it," Kurt said, assisting me with Lee.

"Turn down that light." I pointed to the spotlight above his head. "It's ruining your night vision."

He rotated the rheostat to dim position. "I see something out there, but I don't see any lights."

"There aren't any." I looked back at Kurt, who smiled.

"Moonlight's enough light to land by," I said.

"Are you crazy, Duff," Lee cried out. "This is fucking insane."

"No choice now," Kurt said. "I think number three is about to flame out. Fuel flow started jumping around when you pushed up the power."

We all stared at the engine instruments.

"Protect essential," I ordered.

"Got it," Kurt said, rotating the essential electrical power switch from engine generator number three to engine number one.

"Watch it close," I said.

"Roger," Kurt said.

"Take it easy, Lee. You're doing fine. Just keep her coming down. Everything's going to be fine," I said.

The moon illuminated Lee's face with a ghost-like whiteness and spasms of tension.

I pumped the yoke lightly to gain his attention, feeling the tightness in his arms as he squeezed the controls. "Loosen up. You're strangling it."

He released his yoke, shaking his hands out. "Right, thanks."

"I'm going to push the throttles up a little more so we don't get slow."

Lee shook his head slightly, then whispered something approximating, "I don't like this," or "I'm not sure about this," but he did as the captain ordered him.

"You're flying a good airplane," Kurt said.

"Where's the glideslope? Can you tune me in?" Lee asked.

I chuckled under breath and said, "No glideslope, either." I figured Kurt was probably thinking the same thing: Lee's scared to death. He's never flown outside of the controlled box of airline flying and his discomfort couldn't be hidden.

Lee was silent and his flying became erratic.

"Settle down. I'll talk you through it," I said, getting a little agitated myself. "Give me a thousand feet per minute descent. Can't afford to land long."

"Okay."

"Don't respond, just do what I say."

He nodded.

"Hold her steady. Looking good."

"Five degrees left. Good." A left crosswind had drifted us over to the right of the runway.

"You've got the runway now, don't you?"

He shook his head. Then with a quivering voice he said, "I have the runway."

"You stay lined up on the runway. I'll talk you through the descent."

He nodded again.

"Eight hundred down. Two miles to touchdown. Looking good."

"Seven hundred down. Steady."

"Hold what you got."

"Put in the wind correction."

"Very nice."

"Give me a thousand down. Mile and a half to go."

"Hold it."

"Mile to go, on glideslope. Give me eight hundred down."

"Right there, perfect."

"Hold what you got. Half-mile to go."

"Beautiful. Approaching the threshold."

"Over the runway."

"Break the descent."

"Flare."

"Ease the power back."

The wheels touched the ground.

"Nice job. Get her stopped." Lee landed firmly but safely.

"Good one," Kurt said. "Three in reverse."

"Eighty knots," I announced as he braked moderately to slow the airplane.

I took control of the airplane, exiting the runway at the end. The airport looked to be its usual lonesome self but it wasn't the darkest time I had landed there. A lone light shone from a building on the east side of the airfield, which consisted of a single runway, a narrow parallel taxiway, and an apron midway down. I taxied fast but attentively, aware that running off the narrow taxiway would foil the operation.

"Well done, guys." I looked at Lee, then Kurt.

Lee squirmed around in his chair, wiping the sweat from his brow with his hand.

"Yeah, good flying," Kurt said.

"I'm happy to be on the ground. Are the icing lights still on?" Lee twisted around to see Kurt's panel.

I looked back, too.

"They went out on short final," Kurt said. "It was too late by then. We were committed."

Lee wriggled nervously. "Captain, you sure this was a good idea?"

"Absolutely, safety is number one. We couldn't make Tonopah," I lied, and I'm sure he suspected it.

"Too risky," Kurt said, coming to my rescue again.

"What are we going to do now? There ain't nothing here," Lee said.

"See that light over there?" I pointed to it. "There's a phone over there."

"Yeah."

"Yeah, there's a phone in that shack. I'm gonna call the company from there and ask them."

"Good idea, captain," Kurt said.

"Okay," Lee said. "You've been here before, I take it."

"Oh yeah, with the Air Force Reserve all the time."

"Should we ACARS them?" Lee asked thinking about the data link system of communication we had on board.

"Takes too long to get a response," Kurt said.

"Better to call them direct," I said. "I want to talk to a real person anyway."

Lee, on his toes, suggested, "What about the airphones?"

"I don't want to alarm the passengers any more than they already are. I need privacy, lawsuits and all, you know?" I said, as if I were thinking out loud.

"You're right," Lee said.

I thought about my plan if Lee were to pull out a cell phone, but he never did. I moved the thoughts from reactive to proactive, as I had been trained for command. "Kurt, call Marcia and have her come up here."

He picked up the phone and called her.

"Start the APU, too." I knew he'd already started the auxiliary power unit, but I wasn't yet ready to abdicate my role as airline captain—for Lee's benefit of course.

"Done," Kurt responded gruffly.

I saw the sleek blue Gulfstream V. An orange glow like the coals of a fire burning long in the night came from the cockpit. I taxied close—wings nearly overlapping—and parked abeam it.

Lee pointed cross-cockpit. "You see that airplane, don't you?"

"Yes, I see it."

"You look too close."

Mark A. Putch

I looked back, out my side window. "Looks good from here." I nodded to him. "Remind me to show you something later."

As Lee shut down the motors, Marcia entered the cockpit. "Hi Marcia. We made it," I said.

"Thank God." She took a deep breath.

"How are the people?" Kurt asked.

"They're glad to be on the ground, but they're asking questions, lots of questions."

"Open the liquor bins. Keep 'em lubricated."

"We are."

"Do you have anything to feed them?"

"We have more snacks in back and unfinished meals in first class."

"Good. Brief the girls in back to keep everybody happy. I'll make an announcement to the passengers.

I want you to come outside with me to call the company." I touched Marcia on the arm.

"Kurt, I want you to go outside to see if you can find anything that might have caused the icing lights to come on. Go ahead." I nudged him on the shoulder. He hurried out of the cockpit carrying a flashlight.

"Lee, you stay here with the jet. You're in charge until I get back. You've got to comfort the passengers as much as possible." Lee's experience was best suited to deal with the passengers, I figured. "No cell phones, whatsoever. I don't want CNN to get wind of this before I get the company in the loop."

Lee nodded.

Marcia gathered the flight attendants into the forward galley to brief them.

I made an announcement: "Ladies and gentlemen, this is your captain. We've made an emergency landing at an airfield in Nevada. We had an indication of fuel contamination, but there's nothing to worry about right now, as we are safe on the ground. I repeat, there's nothing to worry about now. I know you're all wondering, what next? I, too, am wondering the same thing. Please remain in your seats while we coordinate with Pacifica officials our next course of action. The flight attendants will serve food and complimentary drinks. I'm asking for your patience, please. I'll keep you posted as soon as I know more. Thank you."

The crew obeyed the orders with efficiency and without protest. Lee worried me though. I knew Marcia had given the flight attendants special instructions to keep cell phones off. A panicked passenger alarming the world with half-truths and speculation would only make the situation worse from a public relations standpoint, she told them. The captain has the final authority on cell phones, they were instructed to tell passengers. We knew it wouldn't work for long: Time was of the essence.

As I unbuckled my seatbelt, Lee asked, "Do you want the shutdown checklist?"

"Take care of it."

Meeting Marcia in the forward galley, I whispered to her, "Let's get out of here."

"After you."

Marcia and I walked briskly through the cabin, deflecting tough questions from worried customers (What about my connection? What's wrong with the plane? Where are we?). We said we were working the problem and would answer their questions soon, and that we'd be underway to San Francisco as soon as possible. "Please sit back and let the flight attendants serve you. Thank you for your patience," we said, acting sincere and honest but pressed.

I glanced at Cluny as we walked by. The image of him under that blanket fast asleep stayed with me for a very long time.

We exited through the aft airstairs. I raised them, sealing off the cabin from the ramp. I felt a sigh of relief, as I'm sure Marcia did, but no words were exchanged.

Bridget—in black garb—appeared from nowhere. She handed us automatic weapons with extra clips and gave a thumbs-up, indicating her logistical responsibilities were accomplished. Words take time, so none were exchanged. Much work remained to do, and everything had gone like clockwork, thus far.

Kurt, his weapon slung over shoulder, met us at the rear of the plane. He touched Bridget's shoulder and gave a thumbs-up. He'd cut the wires to the radios, ACARS, and air-phones, which were located in the electronic equipment compartment.

Bridget had parked a small forklift next to the rear cargo hold of the 727. I jumped up on it and opened the cargo pit. I stared at the money, neatly stacked in 239 twenty-pound boxes, just as the manifest promised.

Bridget operated the forklift while Marcia stood guard.

Kurt and I got in the pit and began loading the money onto the forklift, working at a frantic pace. We sweated profusely. Our wet hands left handprints on the cardboard boxes. My breathing became loud and irregular as claustrophobia set in. I worked faster for fear of suffocating in that black cave. All I saw was Bridget's ghostly face bathed in an ominous moonlight.

We made three trips between the pit and the Gulfstream, which was parked in the shadow of the 727. We loaded the money through the forward entry door, stacking it in precise locations of the business jet's modified cabin.

We worked about fifteen minutes before things went bad—real bad. We were en route to the 727 to get the last load—about fifty boxes—when the lights of a car approached.

"Stop," I said.

Bridget cut the motor of the forklift; it jerked to a stop between the 727 and the Gulfstream. We watched from behind the forklift.

The car parked under the light of the building about eighty yards from our position. I saw some sort of emblem on the driver's door. I got scared, assuming it to be the Nevada Highway Patrol. A lone officer exited the car.

The 727 seemed to amuse him. He ambled up to and around it with his right hand on his hip. We listened to the sound of his heels on the tarmac that seemed as loud as my hammering heart, except my heart pounded much faster.

He paused at the open cargo hold, in view of the boxes of money. He studied the surroundings, focusing on the Gulfstream and the light escaping its entry door, casting a rectangular swath on the tarmac. He approached it cautiously, glanced sidelong at the squad car, then yanked a radio from his side.

"I'll handle this," Bridget whispered.

"Play it safe," I whispered back.

"Officer," she shouted, emerging from behind the forklift.

He jerked in surprise.

She closed in. "Officer, I need your help."

"Yes, ma'am. What's going on?" He held the radio with one hand and clutched the holstered pistol with the other.

"My forklift stalled. I think it's the battery. Can you take a look?" She stood with arms crossed and head tilted.

"What are you doing here?"

"They didn't tell you?"

"No, nobody tells me anything." He put the radio back into its holster.

"Area Fifty-one mission. You know about Area Fifty-one, don't you?"

"Sure, I was born in Tonopah for heaven's sake."

With hands on hips now, Bridget said, "Top-secret transfer of research documents between CIA and Air Force. That's all I can tell you. Your agency should have been notified."

"They sure as hell didn't tell me nothing." The officer, seeming to relax, looked her over. "Who you with?"

"CIA."

"Where's everybody?"

"In the small jet." She pointed.

"I'd better see your credentials," he said, shifting on his feet. "It's procedure."

"Sure, it's right here." Bridget fumbled through a fanny pack until she found a work ID.

I'd crawled to the opposite side of the forklift, positioning myself behind the officer.

"Well..." Bridget saw me. "No, wait. That's not it."

The officer stepped toward her.

I shadowed him. My plan was to gag him and handcuff him to the forklift until we could get out of there. I was in position.

"Oh, here it is." She held it out.

With a flashlight aimed at the card, he bent over to read it.

I jumped him.

"What the fuck," he yelled, getting his gun out before I could get him on the ground.

Bridget swatted the pistol out of his hand just as it reported a loud *bang* and a flash of fire. The pistol skidded across the tarmac.

I was on top of him before I felt the first sting of his knife slicing through me. The raw power behind the thrusting knife was immediate. Between the spasms of primitive force—muscles stretched so hard they're ready to pop; the mixing of blood and saliva; the taste of sweat and tears; and the adrenaline that obliges instinct—between the desperate elements of survival was the surreal suspension of time—and death. Somehow, I remained rational.

With wheezing desperation and ejaculating grunts and groans, the struggle seemed to last forever. By the time I realized the hollow thump I heard was Kurt kicking him in the head with his good foot, I had pumped three rounds into him at point-blank range, his hot blood pooling underneath me.

"Oh, my God," Marcia yelled.

I pushed up from his limp body. My throat was as dry as old leather. I turned my head away and vomited.

"You all right, man?" Kurt asked.

I didn't feel much, although there was lots of blood. "Surface cuts. Nothing deep."

Sobbing, Marcia stood with her hands over her face.

Things got scary real fast. I knew the passengers had heard the shots.

Kurt and Bridget grabbed the officer's arms, dragging the body out of the way.

"Let's get the hell out of here," I said.

Marcia said, "Yeah, I'm scared to death."

"I want the rest of the money," Kurt said.

"Let's finish the job," Bridget said.

We jumped back in the cargo pit and threw the boxes on the forklift as fast as we could. Adrenaline drove me; the shooting seemed a million miles away.

Bridget spun the forklift around and made for the Gulfstream.

Kurt hobbled fast behind.

Lowering myself out of the cargo hold, I saw the aft airstairs extending. Peering up the stairway, I saw Lee and the other flight attendants standing at the top of the stair with the door open. Lee started down the stairs.

"Hold it right there," I ordered. The gun tucked in my belt and the blood all over my white shirt startled them.

The flight attendants made a gasping scream.

Some passengers gathered at the door.

"Stop. Not another step." I pulled the pistol out.

A flight attendant slammed the door, leaving Lee alone. He stood there with his mouth gaping.

"What's going on? I heard shots."

"Forget it." I walked halfway up the stairs pointing the gun at Lee. I wanted to scare him. "Listen, you're on your own, kid. You have a choice: life or death!"

Lee backed against the door, his eyes darting wildly.

"Fly this airplane to San Francisco right now and deliver that heart. You've got a thirty-year airline career ahead of you. Don't blow it now." I shook the gun at him. "I'm finished; it doesn't matter about me."

"But—"

"Drop it, Lee. You're cleared solo. Go to the cockpit, forget any of this happened, and get these people home. There's nothing wrong with the airplane. We made up the emergency. She'll fly fine if you just remember to do everything I taught you. Now, get out of here." I shook the gun again. "I'll close the stairs behind you. Godspeed, kid."

Lee looked back as the stairs began to rise. "Good luck, Duff."

I sprinted to the Gulfstream, where the crew readied the airplane for takeoff. I secured the cargo compartment and raced onboard, raising the stairs behind me.

Kurt had the first engine running and did preflight checks while I strapped into the captain's seat. Taxing away, I glanced out the windscreen, past the shadows of the 727, and saw the squad car parked under the light. I imagined—hoped—its radio crackled, summoning officers to a remote crash site where an emergency locator transmitter barked its bleak warning across a barren landscape.

Bridget sat in the copilot's seat. Kurt stood between us starting the second engine, then buckled into the jumpseat between Bridget and me. Marcia sat alone in the cabin. We finished the before-takeoff checks while taxiing for takeoff. Bridget had already programmed the navigation system.

I felt shaky taxiing out. The airspeed indicator pointed to eighty knots—way too fast for that narrow taxiway—as we sped for the end of the runway. The transfer took thirty-four minutes—four more than planned, but, having built in a buffer, we were on schedule. Pumped up on adrenaline, I didn't have time to think about being tired.

I rounded the corner onto the runway, pouring the coals to her. Despite being overweight, she leaped—stealthily blacked-out—into the air. I leveled off a couple hundred feet above the ground, avoiding the orange clusters of light that twinkled on the desert floor.

Kurt navigated, directing heading and altitude changes as he referenced and cross-referenced between his map, the navigation display, and looking outside. Terrain avoidance was easy: Moonlight illuminated the mountain peaks, the flashing red lights of radio towers stood out, and Kurt navigated with precision. I trusted him and did exactly as he directed. Finally, a chance to relax a bit came my way.

Our route took us well north of Tonopah, mapped out to avoid alerting the Air Force. We crossed the Nevada state line on a course just north of Mono Lake and Half Dome in Yosemite. Flying over the Sierras at two hundred feet above the ground at night gave me a thrill. The scoured rocks—snowless at that time of year—glistened with moonlight. I followed our shadow briefly across the ash-white terrain.

We flew down the backside of the mountains between the spines of two parallel ridges on a southwesterly heading before spitting out over the San Joaquin Valley. I steered away from the lights of cities and towns and even the single lights of farms where possible, but California was too populated to avoid everyone as we had almost done in Nevada.

Once over the flatland, near Madera, I flew the jet down to one hundred feet above the ground. We zipped across the valley at 400 knots per hour, which used lots of fuel, but we needed to cross it quickly. The valley was the most dangerous place we had to fly because there was no place to hide.

Safe on the other side, we used the coastal ranges to mask our position. We hid in the shadows of mountain ridges as we flew southeast, paralleling the Santa Lucia Range until reaching a point north of Paso Robles. From there in a narrow valley, I banked the jet hard right to a heading of due west and held it until going feet wet—crossing from the land to the water— between Cambria and Harmony.

Over the Pacific Ocean, I pitched the jet up to two hundred feet above the water and steered west for five minutes before turning south for the rendezvous point, fifty-five miles west of LAX.

The modified GV had been used by the Drug Enforcement Agency to track down drug runners attempting to enter the U.S., primarily from the Caribbean. It carried more fuel, had a modified wing allowing it to cruise at mach .90, and had more payload capability than the stock GV. It had an advanced avionics package, including an airborne air-to-air radar similar to that found on fighter aircraft, and an advanced communications package used to spy on the drug smugglers with.

We used it to access the communications network at Pacifica Airlines, which allowed us to monitor the progress of their flights by intercepting VHF radio signals and satellite communications. At low altitude—outside of VHF radio contact—we relied on satellite relays. We could only receive information via satellite, not transmit. Transmitting would have revealed our position.

Marcia tried to run the communications package, but she was stressed over the shooting and couldn't do it. Her premise, as had been for all of us, was that there would be no violence. No one was supposed to get hurt. Luckily, she didn't abandon me. I think she rationalized it to be killing in self-defense. As for me, I knew someone was going to die in the struggle with the cop, but it wasn't going to be me.

Bridget went back to the main cabin—leaving the copilot's seat empty, squeezing past Kurt—to help Marcia.

"I can't find anything on flight 1010 yet. They must be using VHF," Bridget relayed to the front.

"Keep trying," Kurt said.

I had concentrated well and my flying was good. My instrument scan was quick and the airplane flew beautifully. She was responsive and powerful and up to the demands I placed on her. Kurt's navigation skills made flying easy for me because he stayed way ahead of the airplane. I didn't have to worry about much—just fly the airplane and let Kurt do his thing. It gave me a chance to get a good feel for her.

None of us had time to think about the money because—truth be told—none of us thought we would get away with it. We all expected to see fighter escort pull up beside us at anytime, forcing us to land at some obscure military base where we would be tortured and thrown in solitary confinement for the rest of our lives.

They would probably keep it under wraps, we figured, as everything had been done with exceptional secrecy. No one individual could figure it out and everybody else, people such as Lee, had to answer to an interested party. We would simply wither into oblivion in some dismal cell, our crime denied the tiniest footnote in the chronicles of criminology.

If the government could kill a president, then surely the government could cover up that a few anonymous citizens slipped away in the cover of darkness with a satchel full of their money. Besides, if money buys free speech—that's what politicians and journalists said, and silence being a form of free speech, then money buys silence, too, right? Surely, they would spread a few bucks around to shut people up. It would be too embarrassing to the government. What would the hard-working, dutiful taxpaying public think? The irony of it all might be too much for them. Our discussions centered on this sort of logic quite often after it was all over.

As we crossed the Sierras, Bridget intercepted three messages sent to Pacifica flight 1497. They read, "Pacifica 1497, contact Oakland Center 132.95," and, "Pacifica 1497, expect thirty minute hold at Modesto," and "Pacifica 1497, wherever you are, may God bless."

"The messages weren't received, according to the tag," Bridget said.

"They think we crashed," Marcia said. "How sad."

I couldn't see Marcia, but I knew she was crying— heard it in her voice.

"It worked," I said, excited as a devious schoolboy. "It bought us time."

It didn't seem to matter to anyone. The shooting had put a damper on our spirits. I tried to block it out of my mind. While the crew seemed plunged in anguish, I felt a void. It was an instinctive thing that just happened very quickly.

We are all capable of evil deeds. Every man has a secret lust to be a dictator ruling his own world like the patriarchal primate dominates his harem. If raw force doesn't deter him, then the power of morality, honor, or—and God knows this is a big one, maybe the biggest—peer pressure will.

I didn't feel remorse, only relief to be alive because the cop would have killed me. I had no choice and it was not the first time, either. It might have been the third, but I know it was at least the second time I had taken a life.

Mark A. Putch

The first time was in Vietnam when I got shot down over the jungle. I was an Army warrant officer flying helicopters out of Da Nang. It was on an extraction run that we got hit. Charlie made Swiss cheese out of us with high-caliber machinegun fire. I survived, having crash-landed the old Huey into a shallow river.

I heard the singe of instant boiling water as the twisted Huey smacked the water. The rotors slapped at the river like mad oarsmen whacking at the sea. Steam billowed up with the river spray, and the smell of burning flesh watered my eyes.

I got out before the rotors beat themselves out against the sandy river bottom. Jumping into the water from the high side, I prayed the wreckage would not tilt over on me before I could get far enough away.

I ran from the bursting flames—heat on my back—escaping into the jungle. My boots and clothes were filled with chafing sand that I didn't feel until much later.

Nobody else survived.

I holed up in the dense foliage for two days—my radio going unanswered—when I spotted a young Vietcong skulking around in the jungle. He wasn't much older than fifteen. I hid behind some trees, peeking between vines and mossy branches onto a grassy gap where the sun made everything bright—almost white.

He stepped into the light ten feet away from me, keying his radio. I could smell his jungle-rotten odor and his face was grimy and sweaty. I do not know what he said, but it had to do with me.

What changed me from prey to predator was looking at his feet and seeing that he was wearing my copilot's boots. Jim, my copilot, kept his dog tags—sheathed in a black plastic frame—laced on his left boot and the boy was wearing boots three sizes too large for him with dog tags laced in the left boot. I was mad as a hornet right then. It seemed that all of a sudden, I knew what war was. I knew why I was there, and the doubt about the war vanished.

I had my .45 aimed at him. He spoke into the radio, and I waited until he released the microphone so the shot would not be echoed over the airwaves.

I took careful aim, firing a bullet into the back of his skull. It killed him instantly, but he stood suspended for a long second before collapsing to the ground, hitting it with a hollow, blood-splattering thump.

The killing didn't bother me; I wanted vengeance for the blood of my copilot. I did not see him as someone's son or as the source of much wartime sorrow to somebody. He was the enemy—and deserved to die. So I killed him as if he were the object of big-game hunting, except I didn't respect him as hunters respect their prey.

I slept in the jungle for two more nights before being rescued, and at times assumed I would die violently like the kid because I would not surrender—ever.

Then there was the trial for murder of my first wife, of which I was eventually acquitted. Only Kurt knew anything about that because he was my best friend and primary character witness. Marcia and Bridget did not need to know about that, I reasoned.

My mind cluttered up when I thought about it, the way it clutters up when I am trying to picture my life before I had a living memory of it, somewhere around four years old. It took so much effort. It was best to leave it alone.

Eldon, old airtight-alibi Eldon, he helped me, too. I'd never doubt it. Surely, I didn't kill her. I wish I could have remembered; *no, I don't*. Well, the story was airtight and it's best to believe it.

I had not formed a feeling about the cop yet. Haplessly, he got caught in the crossfire. I would think about him later, much later—long after I washed his blood from my body.

"Duff, turn to heading one-five-zero degrees," Kurt shouted.

"Right one-fifty," I responded.

"Did you hear me the first time?"

"No, sorry."

"No sweat. We're over the worst part. There're too many people in this valley. The mountains are good cover," Kurt said, pointing to the map.

"I feel naked out here," I said. "There's no place to hide."

"No shit," Kurt said.

"Where are we?" Marcia asked, craning to look over the nose of the aircraft. She had moved to the copilot's seat when Bridget went back to run the communications console, or console as we called it.

"Just crossed the San Joaquin Valley in central California," Kurt said, putting a finger on the map for Marcia to see.

"How long before we get to the ocean?" Marcia asked.

"Eight minutes," Kurt said, reading from the screen of the inertial navigation system.

"Can't we get there quicker?" Marcia said.

Glancing toward her, I said, "I've got this thing going as fast as it'll go." Marcia looked scared, her face the color of biscuit dough. She didn't say anything.

Kurt shouted through the cockpit door. "How's it going back there?"

"I've got something. Hold on a minute," Bridget responded. "Here it is."

She passed up a satellite message to Pacifica 1010 from the company. "It's some sort of maintenance clearance form or something."

Kurt read it. "Okay, everything looks good. Couple of lights burned out in the cabin and a broken flap indicator."

"Is that serious?" Marcia asked.

"No, they'll use the backup indicator," I said.

"Any luck on the clearance?" Kurt asked again.

"Not yet," Bridget said.

Kurt needed the clearance to verify their route and map it out on his charts. He used the expected flight plan route to make his calculations from but needed the actual cleared route to verify.

"Turn right to 255 degrees, Duff," Kurt directed, pointing out the window to a cluster of lights. "That's Paso Robles over there."

"It looks so peaceful," Marcia said.

I banked the airplane sharply to 255 degrees. "Okay, four minutes to feet wet," I announced. No one said anything, but anticipation hung in the air as thick as a fogbank.

After a minute or two, Bridget walked into the cockpit and stood next to Kurt.

"That's it." I pointed ahead to where a line of craggy rocks met the water.

"Oh my God," Marcia said.

"We've got 45,400 pounds of fuel," Kurt said. "That's 700 pounds down."

"Shit." We didn't have any extra fuel. "We'll make up for it in the holding pattern."

"I hope so," Kurt said.

"You think we'll make it, Duff?" Marcia asked.

I didn't know what to say. *Will we make it? God, let's hope so.* "We'll make it, Marcia. We have to make it."

"We'll make it all right," Bridget said, patting my shoulder.

Everybody understood that if flight 1010 were delayed, the mission would be jeopardized. If flight 1010 canceled or took off too late, we had flight 1050 as a backup. We planned to land short of our destination if we ran low on fuel, but we wanted to avoid that at all cost. It would mean losing our cover. We would do everything possible to make it to our destination nonstop. At a point over the Pacific, a go/no-go decision had to be made and there was no turning back after that. We planned to land with 1200 pounds of fuel—an uncomfortably low fuel state, but it was just that tight.

A production GV can not make a fourteen-hour flight, but this one carried an extra ten thousand pounds of fuel in an auxiliary fuel bladder, and the extra weight of the fuel restricted the airplane's payload capacity. After forty minutes of flight—the time it took to get to the coast—we were still a thousand pounds overweight, but you would never know it by the way it flew. Damn, that was a nice jet.

Kurt said the airplane would carry the extra weight easily. He was right. The jet never lacked for power. I'd give her the juice and she'd accelerate—almost like a fighter, throwing on thirty knots in a heartbeat. And she had left the ground in Nevada with such grace and enthusiasm.

Bridget got us the jet through an aircraft acquisition company in San Mateo. She was their accountant and convinced them to acquire it under some accounting scheme that deferred corporate taxes another quarter if the company waited two weeks to take delivery of it—or something like that. In the meantime the airplane was supposed to be repainted and updated to the specifications set forth by the new owners, a conglomerate she had worked for before.

Bridget managed the operation from start to finish. All she had to do to get the *opportunity* was promise the CEO a dinner date, which she wisely deferred until the deal closed. A very sly woman, Bridget was.

In the fight against drugs, the Drug Enforcement Agency needed an airplane with extended range and quick dash capability to run down other airplanes with a wide range of speed capabilities. The airframe of the Gulfstream had to be beefed up in order to carry the extra weight of fuel and avionics. The new owners—

Mark A. Putch

Silicon Valley regulars—planned to use the airplane to shuttle their executives around the world on short notice, sidestepping the frustration and delays of commercial aviation.

"Feet wet," I announced as we hit the coast, the surf leaving a gossamer outline against the rocks.

"I guess we're committed now, Marcia said. "Good-bye, USA."

"Let's hope so," Kurt said with a glance at the women. "I hate the looks of prisons."

I don't think the gravity of the operation had hit us yet, but crossing the coast had a huge psychological impact on us. We were leaving American soil for good—we hoped.

The coastal fog had lifted and a thick overcast at about 10,000 feet hung over the sky just off the coast.

The moon's spotlighting glow disappeared and the ocean turned pitch black—like tar—as we slipped under the umbrella of clouds. Excellent weather for the mission, I thought. As long as we were below the clouds, satellites could not see us. We knew there would be unavoidable stretches—long stretches perhaps—of clear sky where we were most vulnerable, but that was the risk we took.

"Fly this heading for six minutes, then pick up 140 degrees," Kurt instructed.

"Roger." I hacked my clock and climbed up a little, feeling more anonymous over water. "No fighters yet."

A somber silence prevailed. I looked at Marcia, whose doughy face looked a little better. She managed a smile.

"I'm going to change. This uniform is annoying me," Marcia said.

"Good idea," I said glancing over her long, slender silhouette unfolding from the copilot's seat.

Kurt looked at me as if he'd just remembered something, then ripped off his tie and undid the top button of his starched white shirt.

Marcia changed clothes in the cramped bathroom. I wanted to change too but couldn't. Kurt couldn't fly and I couldn't leave the cockpit unless I climbed up high enough to put on the autopilot, but climbing that high wasn't an option. We had to stay below radar coverage. Bridget couldn't fly because she worked the communications console in the cabin, and Marcia didn't know how to fly. I'd just have to leave on the bloody uniform.

PACIFIC PASSAGES

Dried blood covered my hands and they felt gummy, as if I'd dipped them into a bucket of varnish. I felt nauseated. I blocked everything out of mind; there were too many hours left to worry about bloody hands and feeling sick. A very long night awaited.

A rush of excitement echoed from the back. "I've got something. It's the clearance," Bridget said.

Kurt exhaled loudly. "It's about time."

She ripped it from the printer and handed it to him, saying, "Here ya go."

He studied it closely, comparing it against his calculations. "Looks good, they're flying the normal route with just a few minor deviations."

I felt relieved, because at that point Kurt didn't have enough time to plot a new route from scratch.

Kurt read the wind's speed and direction from the INS display and recalculated the course Pacifica 1010 would fly on her departure from LAX. He plotted a dashed line on his map to represent Pacifica 1010's flight path. "Let me know as soon as you see a pushback, Bridget." He touched her hand.

"You got it."

"That'll be the first entry recorded in the time block on the flight log," Kurt said.

"Is this where it is?" Bridget asked pointing to an old flight log they used for training.

Kurt looked down at the paper. "That's it."

Marcia came out of the bathroom wearing shorts and a loose T-shirt.

"Marcia, hand me a bottle of water and a rag, please. I want to clean up."

"Sure." She stood behind Kurt, bending over his shoulder to wipe me down.

Having logged thousands of hours flying low-level, I didn't worry about crashing into the ocean—as long as I kept it steady. The only things out there besides an occasional bird were a few ships and oil rigs. Kurt kept us clear of the oil rigs that he had plotted on the map and I kept a careful scan on the horizon for tall ships, most of which we flew above anyway. Even in the darkness, my eyes had adjusted and I could see the ocean clearly and the area around us relatively well.

The cold rag on my face felt good. Marcia washed the blood from my hands and face.

"Thanks, Marcia." I kissed her arm.

She hugged me tightly around the neck.

Another roar of excitement flooded in from the back.

"Pushback, 0511 Zulu," Bridget yelled up.

"Good. That's only one minute late," Kurt sighed.

"Thank God," I said and slapped the dashboard with excitement.

"Start climbing," Kurt instructed.

"Roger." I jammed the throttles forward and pulled the nose up in a bridled climb. "I'm going to stay below the cloud deck until I have to unmask."

"Good idea," Kurt said. "Give me a 150-degree heading. The wind's pushing us east of course."

"One fifty, coming up. How's the gas?" I asked.

Kurt added up the fuel gauges meticulously. "Eight hundred down," he said dourly.

"Getting worse," Marcia said.

"Damn. We'll make it up at altitude," I said, though I wasn't sure.

"Bridget, you'll be able to pick them up on VHF now," Kurt said. He gave her an airport diagram with the radio frequencies for LAX on it.

"Thanks."

"Monitor 1010's progress on ground, tower and departure control frequencies. I'll plot his course against the template," Kurt said with confidence.

"Okay, he's taxiing to runway two-four left. They're on taxiway Delta," she said, mapping his progress with the diagram.

"I'm going to monitor the frequency with you, Bridget." Kurt adjusted the volume of his radio.

"Okay."

"Do you want to listen, too?" Kurt asked me.

"Yes, tune me up."

Kurt raised the volume of my radio and I heard the incessant chatter of Los Angeles ground control issuing taxiing instructions. "A little higher, please." He raised the volume steadily until I gave him a thumbs-up.

"They're approaching the runway," Bridget said.

"Good," Kurt said.

I climbed up to 11,500 feet, just below the overcast in that area. I pulled the power back to conserve fuel, the high whine of the engines falling to a whisper and the propelling force of the thrust abating with inertia. "This'll help with the fuel," I said to comfort everyone.

"As long as he gets airborne *real* soon," Kurt said.

"Ground control told them they'd be number three for takeoff," Bridget said.

Kurt busied himself plotting the intercept point.

"Change your radio to tower frequency, Bridget," I said, dialing in tower frequency in Kurt's and my radio.

I looked down at the INS display. "The INS says the holding fix is off the nose ten miles."

"That checks," Kurt verified.

I flew a holding pattern designed to foil the radar skin paint return that LA Center would have picked up on their radar. We were not too worried because we knew LA—too busy to bother with uncontrolled traffic—would drop us from their scopes, that is, if they picked us up at all.

"The way the moon is tonight—so bright and everything, I think we should do a low-to-high intercept," I said.

"I think you're right," Kurt said. "I doubt they'd see us if we intercepted them from above, or from any other way for that matter—these guys are blind, you know?—but we don't want to risk it."

"No, play it safe. I'd prefer the energy advantage of having the altitude to trade for airspeed if we go cold. You know what I mean?"

"Yeah, we won't have anything to work with if we miss it. It's got to be...perfect," Kurt said.

I looked at him closely, then let my eyes move to the copilot's seat with a subtle head nod. Kurt moved from the jumpseat to the copilot's seat. I knew it'd be hard for him, but he seemed okay as long as I didn't ask him to fly. Kurt focused on the radar. On the western leg of the holding pattern he turned the radar on to make some checks, and turned it off before I turned back toward shore so as not to alarm any military radar sites.

The success of the intercept depended mostly on Kurt, who had to plot it on his map as the dynamics of the situation developed in real time. We had the radar to help us in the end game but his tracking of Pacifica 1010—a Boeing 747—had to be precise, otherwise we risked joining up on the wrong airplane—or no airplane at all. And not just any westbound airplane would do. It had to be Pacifica 1010—the mission depended on it—because Pacifica 1010 was going the distance.

We had to know 1010's exact position relative to ours. He did it by plotting their course based on standardized speeds and climb profiles and departure routes, updated in real time with air-traffic control instructions. It was a difficult task at best but Kurt could handle it.

We had a few obvious advantages over the 747. It was lit up like a Christmas tree while we ran blacked out. Flight 1010 had no reason to suspect or even dream something like this would happen, so obviously they'd not be looking for us. The hunt was on—the ultimate in big-game hunting adventure of an unsuspecting prey. It was quite an adrenaline rush.

One of our concerns was that air-traffic control would point us out to them as unidentified traffic and they would watch us intercept them, but that was the risk. That was another reason we decided to intercept them from below—they would have a harder time seeing us looking down because of the 747's restricted visibility from the cockpit. We used the belly of the 747 to shield our approach.

We discussed another problem, too. The intercept we'd designed called for a lateral offset, followed by a slow, arcing turn to roll out just behind and below the 747. We did not want to roll out too far behind 1010 because running him down would take time as we didn't have much airspeed advantage and the opportunities for angular cutoff were nil. A transpacific airliner—once on course—does not make large heading changes that we could use to catch him by cutting across his turn radius.

"Bridget, Marcia," I said through the cockpit door. "I need to brief you about the rendezvous."

The women entered the cockpit.

"We're ready," Bridget said, Marcia nodding with her.

"We're going to get really close to the forty-seven. You're going to think we're going to hit it, but we aren't, don't worry. We'll be flying below and near his tail, only ten to twenty feet below. It'll be uncomfortable to you at first, but it's perfectly safe. You'll get used to it." I looked into their eyes. We had covered it before, but I wanted to reinforce it again, mainly for Marcia's benefit. "It's the position the Air Force calls *close trail.* We used it for aerial refueling. It's not bad at all, really, but the intercept might look a little hairy because I'll have to keep my speed up to close in on him all the way into position. I'll probably use the speed brake to control the closure at the last moment and it might scare you, but we can't risk missing the intercept."

Marcia winced again, asking, "Do I have to watch?"

"No, not at all. Wait in the cabin and I'll tell you when it's over. Just don't worry about it, please. Everything's going to be fine." I sounded like a cajoling father trying to talk his kids into a canoe trip over Niagara Falls.

Marcia said, "That's what I'll do then."

"I want to watch but if I get nervous, I'll just shut my eyes, or go in the back with Marcia," Bridget said.

"That's fine. We have to concentrate, so we can't afford any distractions. I probably wouldn't notice anyway as much as I'll be focused," I said.

"I'm going to close my eyes and pray," Kurt joked.

Bridget, having returned to her station, interjected, "Pacifica flight 1010 is airborne at 0529 Zulu."

The businesslike atmosphere resumed as we focused on our jobs. Kurt turned the radar on then off after closely plotting the 747's position. We would use it in short bursts until the endgame so as not to give anyone on the ground enough time to track the signal.

"Bridget, tune in departure control in my radio, please," Kurt said.

Departure control gave flight 1010 a heading of 210 degrees for traffic—a turn we didn't expect. Kurt plotted furiously. They were on the heading for two minutes before control issued a heading of 280 degrees. Kurt plotted closely. The 747 passed through seven thousand feet when departure control sent him to an LA Center frequency.

"Tune me in, Bridget," Kurt commanded.

"Me too, please," I said.

LA instructed 1010 to climb at 250 knots through 15,000 feet, causing Kurt to have to make another course adjustment. "I wish we could intercept him below 15,000 feet while he's slow, but we're too far away," Kurt said as he calculated rapidly.

"Damn, that would have helped," I said.

"He's climbing slower than normal. He'd normally be through 12,000 feet at this point but he's at 10,500 feet right now.

"He's heavy tonight," I said.

"Looks like it." Kurt looked at me, then toward Bridget. "Duff, turn left 030 degrees and climb to 18,000—now. Hold 280 knots. It's time to go." Kurt turned the radar on, adjusting it.

I responded with "Roger," concentrating intensely. I thought of nothing but the task, focused on Kurt's instructions, and gave him my complete trust.

I heard Bridget rustling through the messages on her desk until she found the one she sought. "Here's the weight manifest." She passed it to Kurt.

Kurt studied it briefly. "Full to the gills. Full load of gas and every seat filled." He handed it back to Bridget.

"Good. Then they've got the gas to go the distance," I said.

"Unless the weather craps out," Kurt said.

Silence pervaded the cockpit briefly. It seemed I could count every hissing molecule of air that beat against the windscreen. Tension and anxiety hung on every second that went by.

"Too far, Duff. Come right to 090 degrees. Hold a steady 280 knots," Kurt said. Pointing to the radar screen, he then said, "That's him right there."

Flying his instructions, I glanced down at the radar, seeing a blip descend down the scope. I felt the airplane the way an artist feels the soul—and heartbeat—of his subject; I felt her breathe. Every input I made—no matter how small or subtle—spoke back to me with a palpable response, like the responsiveness of a mistress.

My radio crackled. "Pacifica 1010, cleared on course," LA Center said, taking a one beat pause, then continued with, "Normal speed approved."

Pacifica read back, "Pacifica 1010 heavy, roger. Cleared on course."

"Pacifica 1010, climb and maintain flight level two-eight- zero," LA Center said.

Pacifica 1010 responded, "Climbing to two-eight-zero, Pacifica 1010."

"He's heavy, all right," Kurt said.

I nodded. What he meant was that 1010's crew would have been cleared flight level three-one-zero—the higher the altitude, the lower the fuel consumption—if they had been light enough to get up there.

Kurt studied the radar and his map. "1010 was cleared on course fifty-five miles out of LA. They cleared them to 28,000 feet. Climb now to 25,000 feet, Duff. Pacifica's passing 21,000. We'll catch them at twenty-five. Come right 120 degrees."

I banked the jet sharply.

"They're at eleven o'clock twelve miles, I calculate," he said with increased anxiety.

I looked out through the windscreen at eleven o'clock but didn't see them. "I don't see a thing."

"I don't, either," said Kurt. His head bobbed up and down slowly as he scanned the moonlit sky. "Shit, they're climbing slow. Level off at 23,000. Push it up to 350 knots."

PACIFIC PASSAGES

I jammed the throttles forward and expected to find the looming expanse of flying steel exactly where he said it was. I felt vulnerable above the clouds in the bright sky, throwing radar signals onto the orange bed of Los Angeles. I worried LA Center would detect our presence, but I didn't hear a thing and Kurt said he didn't, either.

"Come right another ten degrees," Kurt blurted. He looked outside, scanning the sky from top to bottom. "Hold the speed right there. He should be at eleven o'clock eleven miles," he said reading from the radar screen. He locked the radar signal onto Pacifica 1010.

"I don't see shit," I said.

"Just hold what you got," he muttered.

Center sent Pacifica to a new frequency.

"Tune us up, Bridget, quick," Kurt said.

Mark A. Putch

I nodded with a side-glance toward her. She had moved up to the jumpseat.

A glissando sounded as Bridget dialed in the radio frequency.

"LA Center, Pacifica 1010, passing flight level 230 for flight level 280."

LA Center answered, "Roger, Pacifica 1010."

"He's passing through 23,000 feet. Start a slow climb at 1000 feet per minute. He's eight miles out," Kurt said. "I still don't see him, though."

I scanned the horizon high and low, concentrating on segments of the sky.

"I saw a flash of light on the left," Bridget said, her voice wavering.

"Where? How far left?" Kurt asked anxiously.

"Right over there above that bank of clouds. Kind of right through that window," she said, pointing across my field of view.

I jerked my head over and saw nothing. I looked at Kurt, his face scrunched up, his eyes squinting.

"I've got him," he said. "He's at nine-thirty, level about eight miles. We're too hot."

Time seemed to come to a lurching stop. I remember thinking that something was not right. What now? I wondered. Just don't panic, I told myself.

"Fuck! The radar's out of calibration. He should have been at eleven o'clock," Kurt said.

I looked at nine-thirty—still nothing.

"Turn hard left to 070 degrees, quick," Kurt ordered. "We need an offset."

I rolled the aircraft into sixty degrees of bank and turned hard for fifty degrees. The force of gravity suddenly doubled. "Hold on, everybody," I said. Bridget and Marcia couldn't handle the steep turn. I heard them moaning when the gravity hit them. (Later, Marcia told me it felt like someone threw a two hundred-pound bag of flour in her lap, and Bridget said she blacked out temporarily because everything went dark.)

"I still don't see him," I said.

"Right off the nose," he said impatiently, his hands twitching as if he wanted to take the controls but couldn't. "Okay, twelve o'clock, seven miles, just above the cloud layer with the moon shining on it."

I hesitated, straining to find him.

Kurt pointed and yelled, "Right there."

"Got him." I felt a shot of adrenaline surge through my body, just like in combat. All of a sudden

I wanted missiles and a gun. I wanted to be a fighter pilot again.

"Keep him right on the nose for another mile and then we go hot. Push it up."

With renewed confidence, I slammed the throttles up and felt—with animalistic gratification—the surge of power. The 747 grew larger and larger in the windscreen, until it looked like a flying battleship.

"Go now," Kurt ordered. "Thirty degrees of right bank and go hot."

I turned toward the 747, keeping the nose of the Gulfstream ahead of his. Kurt timed it all perfectly but it looked like we were going to roll out in front of him—as if I'd turned too early, but that's just the way it looked; it wasn't early. If I had waited until the 747's relative motion stopped moving across our windscreen, that would have been too late; we'd have rolled out too far behind him, with hell to pay to catch up.

I put Pacifica in the corner of my windscreen, which positioned our nose ahead of his and assured a good intercept, and had to climb at about 1500 feet per minute to keep him there. I checked the throttles at max power again. I had 70 knots of overtake but could have used 100. To keep the intercept hot—keeping our nose ahead of his—I had to roll into forty-five degrees of bank—and that is where I could have used the extra speed because steeper turns caused the speed to bleed off—a few times for a couple of seconds that seemed as long as minutes. I avoided using sixty degrees of bank—really bleeding off the speed and making it very difficult to close in—by staying ahead of the intercept and anticipating the dynamics of the developing geometry. (Intercepting another airplane was something you had to get a feel for—to do it right, you know?)

I held the Gulfstream steadily and flew her up into position like a jockey moving his horse up with the pack. I rolled out about 2000 feet behind the 747 with fifty knots of overtake. I'd hoped to roll out closer to him but was satisfied with the intercept. I would have us tucked into position in half-a-minute. From the corner of my eye, I saw the green glow of the radar disappear as Kurt turned it off with a guttural sigh of relief.

I drove her straight in, easing back on the throttles as the gap narrowed. It reminded me of aerial refueling when I flew A-10's for the reserves a while back. I pressed on in until the 747 filled the windscreen and we were safely under its penumbral cover, our speed bleeding off a knot at a time. Piece of cake, I thought, wiping the sweat from my brow.

I was a little rusty but settled in after a few minutes. I kept a cautious distance until the large inputs I made settled down to small, precise, smooth movements: whispering softly into the ears of a living, breathing jet instead of yelling at it like a frustrated basketball coach, wasting precious energy and effort.

When everything dampened out, Kurt said, "Nice job, Duff."

"I couldn't do it without you, Kurt. Hell of an intercept." I was sincere when I said, "Damn, you're good."

"He sure is," Bridget said, draping her arms over his shoulders and nuzzling her head against his. "What a view."

"Marcia," I yelled, "you still back there?"

"Yeah, I'm here."

"You can come up now. It's done." The job really wasn't done; it was just beginning and I still expected to be intercepted by fighters but knew they wouldn't be able to shoot us down as long as we were tucked in tight formation with the mother ship. For once, I had the feeling of having the upper hand on all those who had controlled my life, their techniques subtle but real and circumscribed by social and cultural conformity. For once, I could thumb my nose at McClusky and all the other CEOs that destroyed perfectly good airlines for their own profit. I felt vindicated.

"Wow, I feel like I'm watching *Star Trek* on a wide screen. This is awesome," Marcia said.

"Honey, you're in this movie. You're the star. You don't have to worry about that," I said glancing quickly toward her standing behind the jumpseat where Bridget sat.

"Keep your eyes on that thing up there. You're scaring me, Duff," Marcia said.

"He's doing good," Kurt said, leaning back to see Marcia.

"How about a nap, Marcia? That way you won't have to worry about any of this," I said. That slipped out by accident.

"I'm fine. I can't go to sleep right now. My heart's going like the Indy 500."

I recovered with, "Would you bring me a bottle of water, then?" My mouth felt like leather and my lips stuck together as if I were toiling under an August sun in Arizonia.

"Sure."

I gulped down the water. It tasted very good, as if I had not drunk anything in two days. I thought about not being able to get up to go to the bathroom because Kurt couldn't fly and Bridget had never flown in formation. I saved the empty bottle to use as a piddle-pack like we used in the Air Force on long flights. The A-10—a single seat ground attack fighter—didn't have a bathroom onboard.

My mind wandered off to the long flight I once took in the A-10 to Honduras. A tanker from Barksdale AFB dragged twelve of us down there. The only thing that broke the boredom while we crossed the Gulf of Mexico was watching the different wingmen slide in and out of formation to take a pee—their jets flailing around the sky as they tried to get it all in the piddle-pack and not on themselves. We monitored each other to make sure nothing went wrong. Teamwork was what we practiced. We had a good time on that deployment.

"Steel" almost got us into the war down there when he unraveled a hundred rounds—the A-10 had a big-ass 30mm gattling gun—into a guerilla camp. Some Contra fighter on the radio cleared him in for a *cold* pass over the target. Nobody could remember, but Steel swears he cleared him *hot*. All hell broke loose—the radio exploding with angry voices ejecting clipped words we couldn't understand—and us being grounded for a few days until the investigation was performed.

It took some *real* big-gun diplomacy to keep us out of the war down there after that incident. Rumors of the enemy surrounding the base kept us up all night worrying about an attack. Now Steel, he was a great fighter pilot, and the commander went to bat for him, claiming the cleared *hot* call was a spoof by the enemy. It all turned out okay and that made us happy—especially Varney looking out for Steel.

My yaw damper kicked off over the Gulf on the way home from that deployment. I didn't realize it—although an annunciator light alerts the pilot when it happens—and when I went to refuel off the tanker, my jet swerving around like a pendulum on the boom. The guys laughed like crazy to keep from crying, they'd said. I was a wingman back then and my flight commander, flying in the jet next to me, calmly whispered into my ear over the radio using the deep voice of God, "YAW DAMPER." The airplane settled down once I turned it back on. They laughed—I was embarrassed—about that one for a long time.

Remembering old times seemed to help keep me focused, because so many emotions were churning inside of me. I couldn't get Kurt to fly, and I'd never ask. My job—from the beginning—was the flying. The bathroom problem had been solved. Fatigue hadn't been a factor—yet. Residual adrenaline from the intercept continued to energize me, but that was part of the problem—my body had to deal with the extremes of high levels of excitement followed by long stretches of boredom.

"Bridget, monitor all the messages between 1010 and the company. I don't want to be surprised if something odd happens—like they decide to divert into Honolulu. We've got to be on top of everything," I said.

"Sure, Duff." She went to the back to check the printer, then sat back down in the jumpseat. "Nothing yet."

"Thanks," I said.

"Hungry, anyone?" Marcia asked.

"Starved. What do we have?" Kurt asked.

"Sandwiches, fruit, cheesecake, wine, cheese, to start," Bridget interjected.

Bridget had stocked the airplane with enough food to last a week because we didn't know where we might end up if things went bad.

Kurt asked, "How about a pastrami sandwich and some cheese?"

Marcia nodded, saying, "Sure." She turned to me. "And you, captain?"

"A turkey sandwich with a dab of mustard, please."

"Coming up. Bridget, what would you like?"

"How about some cheese and crackers and you and I drink a bottle of Sirah while the boys fly?"

"No fair," I said.

"Excellent choice, dear. Coming right up."

"Marcia, will you bring me a bottle of root beer, too?" Kurt asked. He smiled at Bridget. "She only buys the good stuff."

"That's right," Bridget said, smiling back at Kurt and stroking his arm.

"Duff, you still thirsty?" Marcia asked.

"No, I'm fine. Remember, I can't go to the bathroom."

"Never stopped you before."

"You're right. Another water will do." Marcia knows me too well, I thought. I needed the bottle to pee in later anyway.

Although I was emotionally attached to her and she to me, I kept a distance she didn't perceive or chose not to. When she stumbled too close, clubfooted and unsure, I appeased her with the diversion of certain attentions she—like any human—craves, steering the intimacy away from the deepest secrets I guarded.

We ate the food; it tasted good. I had not recognized the hunger that lifting 4000 pounds of money caused until we began to eat. There had been no time to worry about food (I don't think I'd eaten all day). So much had happened in just a few hours. My life was changed forever and there was no going back.

Marcia and Bridget enjoyed the wine, the first bottle and then the next and the next—I lost count after that. I measured their intake by the increasing giddiness and eventual idiocy. I didn't need to see the bottles pile up because my mind's eye saw all there was to see. It made them feel better about everything. I listened to them talking about being rich as I stayed close to the 747 in Thunderbird formation—we'd entered some clouds.

I made small, continual movements of the power and flight controls to stay in position, concentrating closely. After awhile I relaxed, thinking about many things and was able to converse the same as Brahms could read a novel while he played the piano, entertaining the drunken clientele of tawdry taverns.

"I don't feel rich. I don't know what it feels like," I said.

"Too overwhelmed to feel rich," Kurt replied.

"Try the wine," Marcia said. "It'll make ya feel rich."

We all laughed loudly. The girls were drunk. I would have been drunk too, I suppose, if there had not been another ten hours left at the helm.

"Down 500 pounds, Duff," Kurt said.

"Moving in the right direction," I said, but we needed more than a couple of hundred pounds for a reasonable safety margin. The gauges had that much error. I started to sweat the landing with the real possibility of running out of fuel before we got there. A lot can happen in ten hours.

Kurt turned to the girls, saying, "Now we've got the same problem as the rich."

"What's that?" Marcia asked with a slur.

Kurt pulled at the sheep's wool on his seatback. "We've got to hold onto it."

"Isn't that the truth," Marcia said.

Bridget snickered. "There won't be any telemarketers where we're going."

Kurt and I laughed while the women became hysterical, one silly joke leading to another until I had to tune them out.

I didn't think of myself as being rich, mixing company with three other recent American millionaires, because there was too much left to do. If we even made it to the island, we'd still have the problem of laundering the cash. The serial numbers on the bills had me worried. The money had to be cycled through a complex, multilayered transaction procedure to avoid leaving a trail. We weren't rich yet, hell no. There wasn't a single twenty-dollar bill we could spend until it cycled through the system.

The banker came to mind. He was a benevolent businessman and finance minister of a cash-strapped island nation in the South Pacific. He didn't ask many questions and neither did we. He guaranteed us a discreet cycling of funds through what he called the dry-cleaning technique—don't ask me what that meant, but I suppose it meant something a little more deluxe than the Laundromat option—for a nominal ten percent fee.

The funds were then disbursed to private numbered accounts in banks around the world. I trusted him but naturally feared he'd want more money in the end, knowing we were at his mercy. It's that feeling one gets just before closing on a house, knowing they might try to add some extraneous charge, but it's much worse because there's no law stipulating truth-in-lending in the international arena. It's a gentleman's agreement backed by a handshake, which is better than any law—until trust gets violated.

The banker had been highly recommended and his anonymity was just as important to him as ours was. I would never violate his trust; I'd probably take my own life first. I met him about ten years ago. Our relationship began with some simple international trading accounts into the U.S. stock market where profits were tax-free. He knew I had connections and I knew too much about his operation, and as he said with a funny accent, "The operation is essential to my country's survival."

My greater fear was our loss of anonymity in the job, but he didn't know where the money came from and didn't care. It would be impossible to pull off a job like ours without the paranoia of being murdered and robbed by some hatchet man, assuming they'd get away with it. We could build in as many checks and balances as possible, but in the end, all we had was trust. We had to play it real cool, keeping our weapons close by.

The women knew what awaited them, but the wine took the edge off. I was glad for them but feared it might be the only time they would enjoy the money. I didn't want them to get drunk, but I didn't stop them, either. The last thing I wanted them to have was a hangover when we got there.

The intellectual payoff to the criminal mind is the realization of earning—well, stealing—more money in a few short hours than the average person could hope to earn over the course of twenty-five lifetimes. No more payroll garnishments—and that's what I considered them to be. No more taxes, insurance, social security, "privilege" fees, union dues, disability premiums, crooked political assessments such as "special workers' comp," child support, and alimony, just to name a few of the ironclad bastions of forced disbursement. It was liberating to think about it—and yes—these assessments were equally as vile and corrupt and flawed as stealing the money. It's one and the same, I thought.

I knew this to be true all my working life, but blocked it out as I had blocked out certain other compromised principles for practical reasons. Compromise, I'd had enough of. The way I saw it, there were two ways to take it: close my eyes and keep divvying up my lifeblood to the looters or do something about it, something bold and courageous, the way advertisers do it on TV; the way they make us all want to do something big—such as scale the statue of liberty in a Dodge Durango. Quite frankly, I thought I deserved obscene wealth because I have such a damn good mind.

Yep, you heard it right. I'm a hell-of-a-lot smarter than most of those rich fucks. Why the hell shouldn't intellect determine the degree of one's wealth? That's what we were taught in school. Nobody ever said they were molding us into clay men—we didn't know that productive citizen meant *governable* watchmen of the elite's wealth and power—of the state, the financiers of burdensome taxes and laborers of a tiered society. Work hard, make money, and make some for me, too. And McClusky of all people, he ain't never gonna get jack from me again, that sorry shit.

I knew that intellect and wealth weren't synonymous—not even in America—but my rebellion was vindication for all those smart guys I knew who didn't have a pot-to-pee in and my success was paradox to the many fools who'd stumbled upon wealth—McClusky being one of them. Why I'd hated the rich, I'm not sure—I guess I hated their arrogance—but to rant and rave over them made me feel better, and it took my mind off the cop.

I can't explain why money was so important to me, but from an early age, I never envisioned my adult life without it. I had a desperate drive to obtain money—lot's of it. Perhaps it was from being so poor growing up. Living in government housing, eating food bought by food stamps, being subjected to the scrutiny of prying cashiers questioning every purchase, saying, "You can't buy that with food stamps," shaking a finger at the only extra joy I ever had in life. (When did a Payday become a felony anyway, bitch?) I'd never live that way again. Hell no. I'd choose death over the undignified life of a hand-to-mouth existence—that's all I ever had with women.

Women cost money—*real* money. Every woman I ever had wanted my money more than they wanted me, maybe because it was such a priority with me, psychologically you know? My first wife, making as much as I did, wanted half my assets. She flew for Coastal Air too, being one of the first female airline captains in the country, yet she wanted so much from me—half of everything. The divorce battle went on for over two years, accumulating huge legal bills. The divorce never went through. She turned up dead.

Cops found her body on a Saturday and the final hearing was set for that Tuesday. They said I did it, but I won an acquittal, thanks to a good lawyer.

Eventually, I got a million bucks in insurance, some of it not available for years because of the suspicion of foul play—even after the acquittal. Funny, those insurance people grilled me harder than the grand jury did.

I lost most of the insurance money when Eldon crashed the King Air, killing one parachutist and crippling another for life. What little money I salvaged went to buy the house I left to Janelle in Walnut Creek, an exclusive area she insisted on.

I didn't kill my *ex*-wife. Eldon made sure of it, but everything seemed a haze: that part of my life blocked out—a blank. I was in his debt big time for the alibi, but I hoped I wouldn't have to see him again—ever. I didn't kill her, couldn't do it—I might have thought about it—but no, I didn't kill her. It wasn't possible.

I started to feel drowsy; my body felt heavy and lifeless. *Oh, please God, You don't think I killed her, do You?—the mother of my son, the son I loved so much—*

Kurt's snoring snapped me out of my black thoughts. I glanced at him, a thin river of silver drool pooling on his shirt. I put my hand under his chin and pressed his mouth shut. He mumbled and twisted around in his seat but kept sleeping. I knew how he felt. The women were still drinking and giggling in the back.

Janelle had asked for everything too but I knew she wouldn't get it 'cause she and a neighbor were sleeping together, and I had proof of it. Rick, the neighbor, treated me like a best buddy when we got together, and that was a slap in the face when my private investigator explained everything. "It's all right under your nose, Duff. Rick's the one fucking her," he'd said.

When I got past the denial, it all made sense. Janelle would spend my whole paycheck before I could get it home. I felt like a personal slave to several credit card companies. After a while, I was totally demoralized and depressed. I even thought about taking my own life—just ending it all. It seemed nobody gave a damn about me. I was just a paycheck; my feelings, desires and needs didn't exist. I was a machine for someone else's use. Once I'd worked through the depression—I'd never really been depressed before, not my nature—I got mad, and the more I got pissed off, the more I wanted to live.

I left Janelle with over $200,000 in credit card debt—all hers—so I felt some vindication. She got a lot more from me than she deserved—I had no choice. I didn't want to alert her that something was up. She got the equity in the house and my retirement account—more than enough to pay off her debts. I didn't worry about her; she'd get by. I figured Rick would marry her—he had the means (owned a big-shot law firm in Oakland). After all, Janelle was a stunning beauty—a real trophy wife.

I couldn't keep Janelle happy because one has to give the trophy wife what she wants—that's the deal going in, everybody knows it. I didn't make enough money. Janelle was beautiful enough to have any man she wanted. An airline pilot just didn't make enough money for her—funny she thought we made a lot more than we did. All I did was beat my head against a wall trying to make her happy, but ironically the only happiness was in getting out of the trap of trying to satisfy her.

The idea of stealing money germinated from the seeds of need as a means of satisfying Janelle's appetite, but it was much later when I understood just exactly what I was doing and why. I knew the plan would free me from the lockdown of middle-class mediocrity—that was a given—but later realized it was just as much a desperate concoction to escape Janelle's deadly trap, too. When I found out about her and Rick, it all came together. For the first time, I understood with a renewed sense of clarity why Janelle wasn't part of the scheme. I recruited Marcia into the plan. Things were different between Marcia and me—mainly because she loved me.

I'd dated Marcia before I married Janelle, but we both ended up making bad choices. I hadn't seen Marcia in years until we flew together a couple years back. She told me about her divorce on the layover, in the bar. We danced. I held her in my arms, comforting her, and wanted to make love to her because I'd always loved her. Nothing happened. We drank a few margaritas and went to our separate rooms. I stayed true to Janelle until I found out about Rick, and then Marcia and I got back together.

Things were simple with Marcia. She never had kids and my son (a missionary, roving between exotic foreign venues) was grown and gone. We fell back in love where we left off a decade before. I was madly in love with her and she was madly in love with me, although the shooting had changed something about her. She suddenly seemed distant and cautious. I figured she'd get over it once we settled into a new lifestyle of romance and freedom.

As much as I loved Marcia, I didn't plan to marry her. I'd had too much bad luck with women. I didn't want to ruin it by placing a gold ring around her finger like a manacle around the neck. I figured as long as we loved each other, we'd stay together, and I'd make love to her every chance I got. She felt the same as I had—a marriage certificate didn't mean anything to her, either. We talked about our relationship all the time.

The money was what worried Marcia. She told me she wouldn't be comfortable managing the large sum of money we expected to get—over eight million dollars each—and asked me to help her. She wanted to put her money in my accounts. I told her she'd have to have her own. I suggested that she hire a financial planner. No longer could I accept—stomach—the idea of financial dependency. It was symbolic, but I wanted her to work it out herself.

I'd always felt—and now had the freedom to exercise my beliefs—that dependency weakened the human spirit and that legalized dependency, such as marriage, was the worst kind because it destroyed the soul. It sounded harsh, but I'd been devastated by the pain and suffering that my wives had caused me. I didn't want to ruin things with Marcia, too.

The way I saw it, she had her money, and I had mine. That was why I felt good about leaving Janelle what little bit of money remained—I still had something resembling a conscience. In my mind I'd paid her off—was finished with her—because killing her was out of the question. I'd already been accused of killing Claire. It wasn't doable. Hell, they would have nailed me to the wall despite any rock-solid alibi or first-rate legal services I could have bought. I could have been on a trip to the moon and they would have accused me if anything happened to Janelle while I was gone. As the cheated-on husband, I'd always be the prime suspect; it just didn't matter. You have no idea what it was like to live in a society that considered you a murderer in spite of being acquitted.

I didn't know what would become of Bridget and Kurt, whether they'd marry or live together or separately, much less what they planned to do with their money. I didn't ask because thinking about it left a hole in my stomach. We (Kurt and I) decided we'd have to split up after the job—when the money cleared—and never look back. I didn't even know what their assumed names would be because Kurt handled all the aliases and legal documents.

He used some complex random process that tracked the records of dead people. The computer made the selections by responding to his software program. He could generate an alias in a matter of minutes. Kurt gave each of us several aliases that we could use in certain situations. He had all the equipment for making authentic documents, too. All those computer classes and all the hours he spent behind a computer screen after his accident paid off, yet it sounded like boring work when he talked to me about it.

I wasn't even sure if I'd stay with Marcia or if I'd end up with Bridget, but I tried not to think about it because I loved them both. (I never met a good-looking woman I didn't want to love.) My mind wandered across moral lines, which gave me two choices: ignore my attractions as I had in the past—living in social shackles—or risk the backlash sure to befall me if I pursued my desires. I respected Kurt, and that respect was the one thing that held me back, but when the split came, I couldn't be sure there wouldn't be some surprises. It pained me to think about it.

I felt guilty for my emotions and deep secrets. They made me feel like a betrayer and someone untrustworthy. I rationalized my thoughts as *truth* and acknowledged my God-given instincts as a man, but I never had the guts to back talk my inner voice of reason: Control yourself, man, you're no animal, I insisted, you're so much more: thinking, self-disciplined, emotionally complex—far removed from the most advanced animals of the earth. The problem, I feared, was that no one really knew just how much I wanted to be an animal. I eased out of that line of thought—left it as prey to cowardice—fluttering around in a tempest of emotions. My head seemed to be spinning on a merry-go-round. I think it was the flying in close formation that got to me.

Kurt looked over, half-awake, and announced, "Seven hundred down."

I looked at the navigation screen, noticing that the winds were stronger than forecast. "Winds are strong," I said, pointing to the bright green display.

"Better keep a close eye on 'em. We'll have to make a decision in two hours," he said.

I glanced at him, then focused back on the mother ship. "I don't want to land in Hawaii. Leaves a trail." I added a little power to catch up with the 747.

"Nope, we'd lose our cover for sure and probably get caught." He put his hands on the dash and leaned forward to study the sky.

"Bridget, can you handle getting 1010's position reports? I'd like to see how they're doing," I said.

"Aye, aye, sir. I'm not that drunk."

"Good," I said.

She separated a long ribbon of messages. "Lots of stuff here."

"Just the most current one," Kurt said, leaning his head through to the cabin. "You girls look bad."

Marcia lifted her wineglass. "We feel great."

"Here it is." Bridget handed it to Kurt.

"Thanks. How's the wine?" he asked.

Bridget snickered. "It's good, how's the water?"

Kurt laughed. "I don't know, but the root beer was good."

"The water's warm," I said. "Come on in."

Bridget laughed as she sat down on the jumpseat.

"I liked the second bottle better than this one," Marcia slurred with a hiccup, leaning over with her arm across my seatback.

The cockpit suddenly smelled like a wine cellar. "Take it easy on the wine, would you? I need you sober. Three hours into the flight and you girls are already drunk. We've got a long way to go still," I said, sounding like a chaperone in Las Vegas.

Bridget pointed a long finger out the windscreen as she said, "Just keep your eye on the road up there, captain."

"I am," I said with a sidelong glance.

Kurt analyzed the report. "They're running consistently low too, about 3000 pounds down."

"Three thousand down isn't much to worry about for a 747. How much total fuel do they have on board right now?" I asked.

"Um, says they had 279,000 pounds ten minutes ago."

I punched in Brisbane in the INS and read off the total time remaining, then made a quick mental calculation with the fuel. "They have enough gas to get there, but they'll have to watch the weather," I said.

Kurt put his hands together and rubbed them. "Good." He'd never checked out in the 747. "Hope the winds don't get any worse. The last thing we need is for 1010 to divert on us."

"Then we're dead in the water," I said under my breath, banking the Gulfstream very gently left to slide over to the left side of the 747's tail section. My neck got stiff holding the same position directly under the tail. The bank was not much of a turn because if I had really banked the aircraft—enough for the crew to notice—we would not have been in formation with the 747, or Whale as we called it, any longer. Our flight paths would have instantly diverged like fighters peeling off their leader's wing, leaving us split-up forever, never to catch her again.

You have to have a feel for flying formation. You have to anticipate inputs, sort of think about making an adjustment then very gently and smoothly move the controls for the desired outcome, striving always for perfect position. The control movements were subtle—never jerky or erratic—and could be as sensitive and delicate as the pulse in your foot resting on the rudder pedals. It was all finesse, formation was.

Formation flying wasn't easy flying, though. One couldn't just fly the airplane into position, throw on the autopilot, then sit back and relax. No, it was continuous work, always moving the controls and the throttles to stay in position. Never a break—one couldn't take his hands off the controls for more than a couple of seconds at a time. The flying drained me emotionally and physically (the constant drone of the engines, the incessant hiss of the windblast taking a steep toll, too).

Kurt read the report. "They're estimating Brisbane at 8:03 a.m. local time, tomorrow." He reset his watch.

"That's twenty-five minutes late. No wonder they're going like a bat-out-of-hell...and burning so much fuel. We'll never be able run with them all the way down there going this fast. Hell, they'll run us out of gas over the middle of the Pacific," I said, abruptly resting my hand on the throttles.

"I know," Kurt said. "All we can do now is wait and see, then make the decision."

Kurt was right, but I wanted to do something—anything—now. In two hours we'd make the decision to press on past Hawaii or land at Hilo for fuel—the outcome we feared most, but we couldn't possibly pass up Hilo if we didn't have enough fuel to make it to Fiji. That would be suicide. "Right, but watch the gas real close so we can establish a baseline of trends. It's gonna be that tight, Kurt." From the way Kurt looked at me when I said his name, I sensed him thinking I was trying to talk him into something dumb.

"As much as I want to avoid Hilo, Duff, we can't risk it. It's got to be right on," he said, the voice of reason seemed to forget the real possibility of spending the rest of our lives in prison if we ended up landing at Hilo. He sounded as if we were making one of the routine decisions we made every day while flying passengers around for Pacifica Airlines.

I nodded at him. His face looked tense in the dim cockpit lights as he looked at me with a strained smile then turned to the maps outstretched in his lap.

I dropped down to a looser formation to get a good look at the sky. I rolled my head around because my neck felt tight. Marcia massaged my shoulders, neck and the base of my skull. I thanked her when she brought us another round of drinks before she and Bridget escaped back to their private party.

The sky was bright and glancing down, I saw that we had already flown past the overcast. The moon splashed a prism of luminous rays through the miles of canyon laid between the glistening sea and us. A carpet mirroring summer constellations swayed atop the placid waters. "Gorgeous sea," I said glancing out my side window, imagining our dark, occluded figure weaving a path through celestial beams of light, tracing a sinister line across the spine of the sea.

"It looks peaceful. Seems foreign, though," Kurt said.

"Yes, but true peace is on the other side...where nothing is foreign," I said.

"You mean where everything is foreign," he said.

"No, nothing," I said, being an optimist.

He held a stern gaze on me for about two beats, then smiled wide. "You're fucking nuts, you know?"

I smiled back and said, "I guess."

Kurt shook his head, then peered out of his side window.

I stretched out some more, raising one arm at a time and rotating it as much as possible in the cramped space. Drinking water helped me stay awake, but it reminded me how badly I needed to use the bathroom. I excused myself, apologizing to the women and asking Kurt to pull the curtain, then relieved myself in the makeshift piddle-pack. At first I felt embarrassed, but Kurt busied himself with recalculating the winds and fuel and the women seemed oblivious as they chatted nonstop in the back.

I kept the plane in that position until it became a strain to look up sharply to the right. I eased her closer to our escort, adding a touch of power and pulling back on the yoke ever so slightly, rising like an elevator. The break reinvigorated me briefly.

Kurt said his calculations looked better but warned, "We'll have to look at it closer to Hilo."

I nodded toward him. A long moment passed before Kurt said another word. He was a bit terse, but a hell of a good friend that I really didn't deserve and wouldn't have had if he could read my mind. It was later—much later—that I realized he knew a hell of a lot more about me than I wanted to admit at the time.

He seemed to understand me as much as anyone could and overlooked my shortcomings as only friends can do. Thinking about this made me feel guilty. The guilt always started with Kurt and worked itself out like a wide-cast net. I didn't know why he was at the center of my guilt. It was as if he were the first person

I ever betrayed, but he wasn't. It had to start somewhere I guessed.

Kurt said, "You're gonna piss off a lot of young guys who looked up to you."

"They don't care about me."

"In a way, you're right."

"Seniority takes no friends. The only person who likes it is number one on the list," I said.

"Yeah, seniority sucks."

I looked at Kurt, the staunch union member, and said, "Seniority, well, I love to hate it—but it works. Why do you think it sucks?"

"I'm not sure. If you think about it, I guess seniority's not the real problem. It's the few senior assholes that don't understand seniority. It's the ones that make you feel like shit because they're senior and you're junior. It's the graceless among us. I hate 'em...the dicks, you know?—the ones with no style and grace. That's what sucks about seniority."

"What's all this style and grace stuff about? You keep bringing it up lately."

"You know, you have it, but many don't," he said.

"There's a compliment in there, I think."

"Yes, of course. You're a great guy to fly with, Duff."

"Thanks."

"Sure," he said. "What really pisses me off is a senior jerk who thinks his seniority gives him a bully pulpit to lecture from. It's as if, just because he's the captain, he's been anointed lord of the airways. There's nothing he isn't an expert on. There's nothing he hasn't done and there's no place he hasn't been. Uh, it's disgusting, ya know?"

"Yes, I do. Unfortunately, Pacifica hired a lot of pilots like that," I said.

"You're lucky, you don't have to fly with them, but I do… did."

What he meant was that I was a captain and didn't have to worry about who I flew with. "Not anymore." I quickly patted him on the shoulder, then put my hand back on the throttles. In that brief time, we began moving too close to 1010. I pulled the throttles back some to arrest the overtake.

He smiled. "Yep, no more egotistical windbags gonna charge their dead batteries on my bill again. The bastards."

"Good," I said.

"Lack of style is the captain bragging to a flight attendant about how much money he makes or the big house he owns or the fancy vacation he taking," Kurt said. "That's what I mean about style and grace."

"It breeds resentment," I said.

"Pilots are our worst enemy."

"I think most Americans are their own worst enemy when it comes to discretion. I saw it all the time when I was flying to Europe—I'm not bragging here." I glanced at Kurt.

"I know," he said laughing. "Don't be silly. I've never heard you brag."

"Anyway, it's just typically American to flaunt your wealth," I said.

"Might be, but pilots are the worst. That's all I know. That's what I see everyday."

"We'll just have to be more discreet in our worldly adventures. Don't want to give away to the wrong person that we're Americans," I said.

"Yep, discretion, that's what we'll have." Kurt offered his hand and I shook it real fast before I had to change power settings. "Like I said, you have style and grace and that's why junior pilots liked flying with you, me included."

"That means a lot coming from you, Kurt," I said and meant it. "Aren't you senior to me though?"

Kurt replied, "I didn't say I was junior to you. I said I liked flying with you."

We got a good chuckle out of that.

"What's so funny up there?" Marcia yelled.

"We're just laughing about my flying."

"At least you're awake," Marcia said, then her voice reentered the chirping fray as she and Bridget were back in their lively chitchat.

I realized that much of Kurt's bitterness came from his having to sit at the engineer's panel all those years after the accident. It took its toll on his outlook, and frankly, I knew that many of the captains he had to fly with treated him badly. Kurt told me he genuinely hated many of the pilots he'd flown with for their assault on his sensibilities and their lack of what he called *style* and *grace*. I felt bad for him, but all that was behind him now.

My flying had been precise all night, but I started feeling tired—really tired. I didn't know how much longer I'd be able to hold on, and that was bad because we hadn't even passed Hawaii yet. I was uncomfortable. My neck felt stiff, as if it had been in a brace for a month, and I felt sweaty and sticky with the bloody shirt clinging to my skin. I just wanted to go to sleep and forget it all, but I couldn't. Thinking about things kept me awake.

I thought about the intercept because I was proud of it. I don't want to sound egotistical, but I wouldn't be honest if I didn't tell you it was nothing short of artistry. It would've made the boys at the schoolhouse very proud. (They had to be careful what they put in the manuals because some of us could actually outfly textbook standards, making perfection routine with mastery. Then we'd look for greater challenges and that was dangerous.) I saw flying from an artistic point-of-view and despised the technocrats of aviation—those pedagogues who'd spout off arcane rules and regulations, dubious numbers and formulas, and trifling do's and don'ts—as much as Kurt hated the graceless.

The G-five we had was a nice—extraordinarily nice—jet. The engines she had pushed out an extra 12,000 pounds of thrust compared to stock engines. It was faster, too. We were doing Mach .86 across the Pacific, but the extra speed cost us in extra fuel burned.

"Did you ever fly with Pete Sheffield at Coastal?" I asked Kurt.

"I don't think so."

"I flew copilot for him. He's one of those guys that didn't have a lick of style in the airplane, but he knew how to have fun on a layover. Pete was a little older, but he had a way with women. They were drawn to him like a magnet. He kept his hair bleached blond and dressed in Dockers and deck shoes all the time, didn't matter where we were or the time of year. He wore a load of gold around his neck too, even when he flew, he'd have at least one gold necklace on, and

Mark A. Putch

he always smelled like a men's cologne shop." I glanced at Kurt. He smiled and drank from the bottle of root beer. "He had all the right stories too, living on a forty-foot yacht in Lauderdale with a girl half his age and all the kids they had. He loved those kids, I remember that, always showing me their pictures. He told women he had an open marriage and his wife understood the pressures of living on the road. I don't think he ever married her, officially I mean. It sounded better that way, and the women swallowed the bait every time. I guess it made them feel better about it, 'cause they all wanted to sleep with him anyway. These weren't prostitutes, either. These were fine women. Sometimes it could get a little hairy flying with him to places like Rio and Bangkok and Amsterdam because he expected you to have just as much fun as he did and that was bad for more than one marriage. A lot of guys wanted to fly with Pete but not too often. They'd get scared; afraid their wives would find out. I flew with him a lot after Claire." I didn't want to say *Claire*, but it slipped out.

Kurt knew all about Claire, but I wanted to avoid talking about her to him. The women didn't hear me say her name. I thanked the wine for that. They knew I'd been married before Janelle, but I never discussed it with them, much less the trial.

"Sounds like, ah…an interesting guy."

He must have been thinking of Claire. He knew her well and liked her until the divorce because I told him everything. He'd been my soul mate during that time, through the trial and all. I left Kurt to his thoughts, twisting in my seat, sliding the curtain back and asking Marcia for another bottle of water. She looked sleepy and drunk. The girls' party had died down.

I rubbed her shoulder as best I could while trying to stay in position after she brought up the water and a clean pullover shirt. With her help, I unbuttoned the bloodstained shirt and slipped it off, our airplane bobbing around as I hurriedly changed. I put on the clean shirt, feeling refreshed after Marcia wiped my face—numbed by fatigue—with a wet rag. I kissed her hand and her freshness stayed on my lips throughout the long, delirious night. I talked her into taking a nap for a few hours because she needed to be fresh later. "Good night," I said, but she must not have heard me, because she said nothing as she left the cockpit. I got the airplane back into position.

Kurt looked into the cabin. "Bridget's asleep at the console," he said. "I'll be back."

"Take your time."

I began thinking about my airline career and the disappointment it had been. Coastal had been such a great airline to work for until the sharks in suits took over, driving it into bankruptcy. Pacifica was never as much fun as Coastal but everybody thought it would last, but with McClusky selling off assets, it was just matter of time. I felt good about it in the end though, because I'd gotten the last word on McClusky. I'd beaten him to the punch line.

Airline flying couldn't hold a candle to the excitement of flying in the military, especially the Air Force. Flying in formation with the 747 reminded me of military flying. As long as I could stay awake, I loved it. I enjoyed the Air Force better than the Army.

I liked airline pay better than the military's, but the cities where the airlines were located were some of the most expensive places in the country to live.

One of the things that took me over the edge, besides Janelle and McClusky—oh yeah, and Rick, was this feeling of being trapped in a dead-end life. Expenses were so much higher in the civilian world than what I had been used to. I grew to resent it. I began to see life as a burden. I felt burdened to pay off all the scoundrels from my paycheck before I ever got to see it. Initially, it chipped away my spirit subtly, then—when I opened my eyes—I found myself oppressively and maddeningly stripped of a soul. I felt like a piece of meat. My buying power—impressive on paper—had been eroded to that of another middle-class stiff living a mediocre life, working to survive. I'd not bargained for that.

Then there was Janelle and she complicated things tenfold. All she knew was how to spend money like there was no tomorrow—truly. Here I was, an airline captain—one of the best jobs around—yet living a hand-to-mouth existence. I was no better off than the average working stiff making $30,000 a year, and living in California of all places.

I found out that the government loved my job because all my wages were fully taxed. My W-2 could've been hung up on a bulletin board in the post office (everybody seemed to know my salary anyway) because I couldn't shelter a penny of it the way my neighbors that were businessmen did. They would purchase all kinds of exotic, tax-deductible toys. I never understood how all that worked.

My job was the kind of job politicians vied for. I guess because it paid the government so well. I became a mortgaged instrument of the state, lining their leaky coffers for the privilege of being a full-time member of the middle class. Hell, I couldn't blame Pacifica for the system, but I could blame—and hate—McClusky plenty.

I just had higher expectations, that's all. I wanted to get ahead, build some wealth and reputation. I never intended to leave this world as poor and as naked as I came into it, rotting in dank dirt, leaching piss in a cheap polyester suit. I thought there'd be more to it. Why does life have to be so shallow—and confusing?

My journey had been to try to make some sense out of the human train of endless track, but I ended up feeling that I had boarded the train at some obscure station and would be forced off in some other isolated depot in the cultural line, giving up unreserved seats to general admission heirs, paying my debts—always debts—out the door, and backing quickly against a barren landscape to avoid being run over by the speeding train. You see, my outlook had been poisoned—and I was an optimist. I had to get out before I spiraled down to death, an indecent death I feared most. There was no choice to be made for me.

I knew I'd miss the flying though, and it was the *flying* as a young boy that planted a seed that grew into a live oak of passion. The Vietnam War had heavy fighting in those days and when I graduated from high school I joined the Army to fly helicopters rather than risk the draft as a grunt fighting on the ground. After the war, I went to college on the GI bill and about the time I graduated, the Air Force came out with this cool

Mark A. Putch

plane called the A-10. I joined the Air Force Reserves to fly it.

After a few years working full-time for the reserves, I hired on with Coastal Air and thought I'd finally arrived, having fulfilled boyhood dreams. I moved up pretty fast and made captain in those last couple of years before the sharks sent Coastal to the grave. I was still idealistic, having just whetted my appetite for command as a captain. I was married to Claire—she made captain too—and we were making some real money back then until it all unraveled.

I was back at the reserves full-time during the trial until all that was cleared up. I couldn't apply for an airline job until the acquittal verdict came down, then I got back into the airline game. With Kurt's help—remember Kurt was one of my copilots at Coastal—I got hired at Pacifica, which had always been a better airline—financially speaking—than Coastal.

I was thirty-eight when Pacifica hired me, and I realized I'd never make it to the 747 (highest paying equipment) before reaching sixty years old (mandatory age retirement). I'd never have enough seniority. I found happiness at Pacifica for awhile because they made me a captain on the 727 after just six years, but that was as good as it was going to get. It took awhile for everything to go south again, but once I became prey to Janelle's Venus flytrap, it all ended. I simply couldn't make it at Pacifica with Janelle's spending habits, and it was Janelle who really sent me over the edge. All the other anger and resentment spawned—mushroomed—from my unhappiness with her. All the pent-up frustrations of my life came to a sudden boil, as if I were a human volcano ready to blow.

I began to feel drowsy again. My body felt numb all over. The engines and the windblast put me in some sort of trance. I fought against the inexorable tug of sleep by pushing my feet hard against the rudder pedals to get the blood flowing, and I poured water over my face. That helped for awhile.

Pacifica 1010 made a shallow turn to the left. I concentrated on flying in good formation. That perked me up, but it made me dizzy again.

"Kurt, what's going on back there?" I asked, directing my voice into the cabin.

He walked into the cockpit. "I just needed a break."

"Feeling better?"

"Yes."

"How's Bridget doing?"

"Sleeping. Both of them are sleeping," he said yawning.

I wanted to ask him to fly, but I knew just the mention of it would have given him the shakes. The flying was my department, but I was getting so groggy. My eyes were red and burning—dry and in need of rest to lubricate them—from sleep deprivation.

"We're down 1200 pounds." Kurt stood as he read the gauges.

"That's too much."

Kurt said, "We can't make it that low," as if he had given up.

I looked at the winds. They were seventy knots stronger than forecast, unusual for that time of year. They seemed to be getting worse all the time. "The wind's killing us."

"I know."

Having decided that we didn't have enough fuel to make it to our destination, we discussed our options. We would have to either land at Hilo or Nandi, Fiji. In either case we would lose the vital cover of flight 1010. We had already accepted that reality. The question was how long could we hold on to it.

If we landed at Hilo, we would have to fly the remaining distance to the destination at high altitude because our island was too far from Hilo to fly low to (not enough fuel), and we would risk the possibility of being tracked on radar. The other problem with Hilo was that it was still on U.S. soil and we feared we would get caught there.

If we made it to Nandi, a place none of us had been to but were prepared to go, we'd risk leaving a trail too close to our destination, just a few hundred miles from

Fiji. From Nandi we would have enough fuel to fly at low altitude, avoiding radar once we got out of Nandi airspace, but navigation to the island could be difficult if the INS were to fail. Then we would need altitude to help us to find the remote island, increasing our chances of being detected. The island had no navigational aids on it.

Overall, we preferred Nandi as our refueling point, but the obvious problem was that we were not sure we had enough fuel to make it there. Aside from what the strong headwinds did to our fuel, Pacifica had been dragging us across the pond between Mach .86 and .88, a speed that siphoned off our next-to-nothing fuel reserve. All I knew and hoped for at that point was that if we flew past Hilo, we would be committed to going on to Nandi.

"We still have another hour to make the decision," I deferred.

"I know, but I'm worried."

I was worried, too. The gravity of the problem roused me to a higher state of concentration. We studied 1010's position reports and they were battling the same issues, except they had plenty of fuel to make Brisbane so long as the weather forecast held up there. We studied weather reports carefully too, because if the weather in Brisbane worsened, Pacifica would need an alternate such as Sydney or Melbourne, requiring more fuel reserves. They would be forced to refuel in either Honolulu or Nandi. The issues were complicated by laboriously filtering the mental process through the dual strainers of fatigue and uncertainty.

"I'll get Bridget and Marcia tucked into the sleeper chairs, then I need to get some more reports," Kurt said. He looked at me as he crawled out of the copilot's seat. "You okay up here?"

"Yeah, no problem," I said, which was the truth and a lie all at once.

Kurt entered the cockpit with a handful of papers. He shuffled through the sheets until he found the wind data and weather charts. He studied them closely.

"I'll work the console," he said.

"Good. I'm okay, really," I said glancing back at him with a nod.

After a few minutes, he leaned around the cockpit door to tell me he could not get anything on Pacifica 1050, the Sydney flight, or any other flights in the area. Pacifica 1050 had taken off two hours late and he had misplaced the radio frequencies for the other airlines.

"I'll try scanning some frequencies."

"Okay," I said.

We had to stay in the receiving mode only, maintaining strict radio silence just as Japanese pilots did approaching Pearl Harbor. Kurt monitored Honolulu Radio, a weather station, as we neared Hawaii, attempting to eavesdrop on any aircraft requesting weather information. There was not much going on at that hour, only silence, synonymous with the penumbral blackness painted over us by the mother craft and the dizzying flash of her rotating beacon light and her regular winks from the strobes on the wing tips.

Kurt leaned into the cockpit and said loudly, "Nothing."

"Keep trying it," I said, feeling but trying not to sound tense.

"It's useless."

"Nothing up with 1010, either?"

"No, I think everybody's asleep up there," he said.

"Talk about the blind leading the blind," I said, feeling a bit lighter.

"You got it."

I looked at the winds that had been climbing steadily. "We've got a hundred knots on the nose up here, man."

Kurt returned to the cockpit and stared at his calculations with a look of bewilderment. He calculated the data repeatedly using his navigation computer. He toyed with air temperature, the winds, true airspeed, gross weight, fuel flow, you name it. He checked and tweaked and checked and tweaked until he looked up at me as if he had just lost the battle of Waterloo. "We're fucked," he said. "We're gonna have to land at Hilo. We can't make Nandi."

"How bad is it?"

"We'll become a glider about forty-five miles north of Nandi."

"Shit."

"We don't have a choice, Duff."

He was right. A somber spell seemed to be cast over us at that instant. All optimism had been obliterated with this one blow. My thoughts were suddenly filled with images of prisons and the antiseptic stench of death row singed my nostrils. The smell of burning hair came to life in my mind. I was scared, more scared than when the cop had tried to slice me up.

"Check the Hilo weather," I ordered.

"I'll see what I can get. We're too far out to get the ATIS (automated terminal weather information)."

"Fine, just keep checking." I felt self-conscious about my dictatorial demeanor—that image of style and grace in Kurt's eyes—because Kurt didn't need me to tell him the obvious.

Kurt shuffled some papers around, then said, "Kona's good. 1010 checked it along with Maui and Honolulu, which are all good. Hilo should be good too according to this old report. Just some scattered clouds at two thousand, good visibility, and a breeze off the ocean. Shouldn't be any worse than that."

"Good enough." I sure as hell didn't want to go to any of those other places. We chose Hilo because of its remoteness and it had a fixed based operator (FBO) on the field that had fuel available twenty-four hours a day. Hilo, we guessed, would be our safest place in Hawaii to land, and it was the closest airport along our flight path (Pacifica 1010 steered us along a course that would take us about a hundred miles southeast of the Big Island, which is where Hilo was located). Kona was our second choice, and Maui and Honolulu were to be avoided at all cost.

We were about two hundred miles off the coast of the island of Hawaii when we entered an area of turbulence similar to severe windshear. I had to concentrate hard on flying formation because we were being tossed around like a skiff in a squall line. I backed out a bit to keep from hitting Pacifica, but too far back and it was like a whiplash effect, so I stayed fairly close.

The bull ride lasted nearly ten minutes and while we held on for dear life, Kurt said he watched the winds shift wildly somewhere between 50 and 160 knots and that their direction would reverse every couple of seconds. I had never been in winds like that. It felt as if we were flying around in a wind tunnel. We felt and heard the wind shoving against the side of the airplane. The poor old Gulfstream—pitching, creaking, and rocking—took a beating, as did my nerves.

I didn't have to say it—couldn't say it—but the encounter solidified the decision to divert; that is, if we survived it. Kurt had managed—without my noticing—to get himself strapped into the jumpseat in the cockpit. I didn't know he was there until the Hilo weather broadcast started coming in on my radio, because he had dialed in the frequency. I managed to thank him. The report said Hilo had clear skies and eighty-four degrees (it said a lot more, but that's all I heard). I wanted to talk to him about the maneuver of peeling off our escort's wing and thought we would need to wake the women to brief them on Hilo but couldn't. I was riveted to the task of staying in formation and was just about to bank away from Pacifica—without the luxury of words and briefs—and aim the jet for Hilo when something amazing happened.

The windshear stopped. I was dazed for a few seconds until it suddenly dawned on me—Kurt realizing it too—that we had flown through a weather system and were on the other side, now the beneficiary of a strong tailwind.

I pointed to the INS display. "Do you see what I see?"

Kurt said, "What, a miracle?"

"It's unbelievable. Hundred knots on the tail," I said. "Just like that."

He shook his head in disbelief. "It's steady, too."

"The gods are with us, after all."

Kurt went back to work with the computer. His numbers showed that if the tailwind were to hold up for two hours past Hilo and if the winds after that didn't become any worse than forecast, we'd make Nandi with a margin of safety. If the tailwind were to last five hours total, we would make the island.

Because we had little choice—making a decision on flimsy criteria that would never meet the standards of airline flying—we pressed on with the option of returning to Hilo if the tailwind stopped. It was as much a life-or-death decision as is triage. We would salvage what we could of the mission, but ditching in the ocean became a real possibility. We risked it all to avoid stepping on U.S. soil again. We were surely risk-takers with no reason now to give up, I thought, encouraged by a change of fate, savoring renewed confidence, winking back at optimism, the constellation above.

Twelve minutes later I watched—in glances—the hazy, yellow lights of Hilo slide out of sight from beyond the right wing. Lights, any lights, seemed foreign and out of place after flying nearly six hours over the lightless ocean. We're committed, I said to myself. We're going to finish the marathon.

Kurt stared out his window as the last stretches of the homeland passed by, fading away like yesterday. I imagined that he was feeling the same as I: nostalgic, scared, and perhaps lonely; the weight of the operation sinking in on the emotions.

I was glad the women slept, having drunk too much and their being exhausted from little sleep in the past few days—same as I, I'd assumed. Besides, I preferred not to subject them to the anxiety of watching the last vestige of America pass by. Who knew what the emotions of a woman might demand once she understood what this really meant?

Marcia worried me the most because I felt she was in love with me more than she was in love with the idea of completely changing her life. I feared she was the weak emotional link in the operation because I had asked her to join us late in the planning stage. Unlike ours, her decision didn't quite have enough time to congeal, becoming integral to her psyche. Marcia had many grievances with the status quo, but she couldn't articulate them without my help, so I knew she did not fully understand the ramifications of her decision. The feelings were there in a real way—she told me that—gnawing away slowly like termites eating a forest, but I didn't think she had identified the exact problem. The three of us gave Marcia a lot of coaching before we asked her in.

Ultimately, she had deferred to me as a final authority, which I liked and disliked. I liked her trust but I wanted her to be as passionate as I about all this. I needed that reassurance of her commitment, but after the shooting, I could not be sure of anything. I didn't want her to think of me as a ruthless murderer. I wanted to find a way to renew her confidence in me, but it hurt my head to think that way; it would have to wait.

Bridget was different. She had a sharp mind like Kurt's and mine. She understood everything, better than I did. I thought about that for a few minutes and realized I had been unfair—the way I said it, I mean. (I don't want you to think I thought Marcia was dumb.) No, Marcia was bright, very bright. She knew more than I gave her credit for (she knew things about people and feelings and emotions and those things that can't be measured with a ruler). *Shame on you!* I could not pigeonhole her into some stereotype—ditsy blonde or dumb flight attendant—the way so many men did, but control was vital to them—white men, I'm talking about. I started feeling confused again. I must have been thinking too much. All I needed to worry about was keeping the jet in formation, but I had to keep thinking about stuff I did not really know about. *Forget thinking; just fly the damn airplane—*

"I'm going back to check for messages," Kurt said, lifting himself out of the seat with his good leg.

"Good idea."

Kurt came back up with another stack of papers. "Here it is. Pacifica 1010 redispatched to Brisbane. Looks like they're going all the way, too."

"It's a little early for a redispatch," I said. "I guess the dispatchers are confident the weather will hold up."

He looked at me. "Now, we're all committed."

"We're committed, all right," I said firmly, nodding. We really were not absolutely committed—we could always return to Hilo—but I felt confident again. Somehow I knew the tailwinds would hold. In my mind at that point, the only relevant decision was whether we would have to land in Nandi or could we make it nonstop to the island.

Smartly, Kurt calculated a turnaround point from Hilo just in case the wind gods changed their minds. That point, an obscure point in space designated by strange coordinates of longitude and latitude, would be part of our consciousness until we passed it.

My mind's eye saw success on the horizon, a far cry from the gloomily dark prisons it had conjured up just a half-hour earlier. Optimism prevailed for the next couple of hours. With the tailwind averaging 110 knots, making Nandi looked like a sure bet.

Five hours out of Nandi—a little over six hours to the island—I told Kurt to go back and sleep. "I want you to be fresh for the landing."

"You sure about that? Don't you need me to keep you awake?"

"No, I'm okay. I'd rather you be alert for the landing. Besides, I'll need your help finding the island."

"See ya in a couple of hours, then," he said.

I didn't really get sleepy until after the first hour. I took a pee in the water bottle Kurt handed me just before he went to bed. That seemed to take ten minutes. I stretched out against the controls like a cat stretching with an arched back and deep yawn, flexing the muscles in my back, arms, legs and stomach. That worked for a while, and flying in and out of clouds required my utmost concentration to keep up with Pacifica.

I had to be very careful not to go lost wingman—that's an old military term that meant losing sight of the leader and having to follow a procedure to keep from running into him—paying close attention to the Pacifica. I kept the 747 steady in the windscreen, modulating the power and massaging the controls lightly to stay in position.

Sometimes I had to work hard—nearly in a sweat. I would get dizzy when the clouds wisped by, everything a gauzy haze, the leader fading in and out through dark clouds, but eventually we were in the clear and things got boring again. I would then back out a little to take a break between cloudbanks.

Our fuel situation had been steadily improving until we were actually ahead by a couple of hundred pounds for awhile. The winds had paid us back in fuel. The fickle gods were again our friends.

The airplane purred along effortlessly, content as a marathoner clicking off easy miles, sustained by second wind. Pacifica had climbed up to thirty-six thousand feet and pulled the speed back to a comfortable cruise, which helped save fuel. I found myself sustained in a serene hypnotic trance and wanted nothing more than *sleep, sleep, sleep.* I pulled myself out of the abyss, and the only way to stay there was to think about things I knew.

When I concentrated on my experiences flying the A-10, I had the best chance of staying awake. The key was not really the A-10, but concentration itself, so I concentrated on concentration.

Concentration was what it took to be a good A-10 pilot—I mean good at dropping bombs and shooting the gun—back before they put all that high-tech stuff on it. We would slow the process down to one video frame at a time. That is how we learned to do it—using video. We would study our gun camera film closely. After awhile we'd be able to detect—the difference being just one frame sometimes—between deadly accurate and wildly slung bombs, doing little more than making racket and moving large mounds of mud. Strafing took the same kind of concentration. It was all finesse, nothing abrupt or jerky.

I missed flying the A-10, but I never got to take the old warbird into battle. I had been an instructor and taught many younger pilots who would go on to fly in combat. Those things I had taught them were carried on, as they would teach them to others, and somewhere, someone I had taught would test the knowledge on the battlefield. That was something that made me proud; it gave me a sense of connection to something significant.

I concentrated on the techniques of strafing and bombing. I spoke the words in my head just as they had been spoken to me twenty years ago. I went over all the different types of bomb deliveries and patterns, strafing techniques and the different kinds of bombs we used back then (before smart bombs). Going over all that stuff helped me stay alert, and what fun it had been to reminisce about an old love.

I wiggled my toes against the rudder pedals and checked my hands for total relaxation, making light movements of the controls to keep in precise formation. My flying was second nature, not thinking too much about the task. I felt relaxed.

I thought about the technocrats of aviation who lived by formulas and tables and academic wisdom. How I despised them and vowed never to become one. I taught my students to rely less on book theory and more on developing a good style of bombing and strafing and to approach the art with boldness and confidence, but to always execute it with chivalry and finesse. My concern was their survival, not filling their heads full of pedagoguery.

I thought about lots more until I began thinking too much. I drank another bottle of water. I was flying the GV smoothly, continually anticipating the subtle inputs of good formation flying, but then something bad happened and I cannot tell you how it happened. All I remember was this feeling of calm and inner peace—it was a stupor I guess—until Kurt startled me.

"What the fuck is going on, Duff," he bellowed.

"Shit man, you're scaring me," I said.

"What's your heading?" he asked.

I glanced down at my heading indicator, the 747 barreling through a tunnel of black. "Looks like…ah…how can that be?"

Mark A. Putch

"Fuck, we're headed back toward Hawaii," Kurt said.

I compared my heading indicator with the copilot's heading indicator and the INS. "You're right."

Bridget entered the cockpit. "What's the commotion all about?"

Kurt put his hand on her arm. "Something's going on up there. Pacifica has turned back."

Before anyone could tell her, Bridget said, "I'll check the messages."

"Good," I said. "That's what I like about you, Bridget."

She stared at me, and said, "You okay, Duff? You look awful."

"I feel bad, too." My eyelids felt as if they weighed a hundred pounds each, and my hands and feet felt welded to the controls. I released them one hand at a time, stretching and clenching, shaking them out. Everything felt sticky.

"Keep an eye on him," Bridget said, rushing out of the cockpit.

"I will," Kurt said. "Pacifica must be having an emergency."

"Shit, how's the fuel?" I asked, having forgotten about it.

He studied the gauges carefully and plotted our position. "We're down a thousand pounds...and going the wrong way."

"Can we make it to Hilo?"

He calculated again. "It's tight, real tight. The headwind—"

"They've got a medical emergency going on up there," Bridget yelled forward. "They're going to Honolulu."

Kurt wriggled in his seat. "I don't understand. We're closer to Nandi by almost an hour."

That didn't make sense to me, either. "Dispatch must have told them to go to Honolulu for some reason."

"Maybe the medical facilities in Honolulu are better than what they can get in Nandi."

Bridget walked into the cockpit with a stack of messages. "It's all right here."

"What's the problem?" I asked her.

She shuffled through the papers. "An eighty-two-year-old lady sitting in seat 16C passed out into the aisle. An EMT on board says her breathing is irregular and he thinks she had a heart attack." Bridget sat down on the jumpseat.

"Anything in there from dispatch or medical telling them to go to Honolulu instead of Nandi?" Kurt asked.

"All I see is the passenger's name on this one: a Mrs. Dottie Cranbrook traveling to Cairns. Let's see. Pacifica doctors instructed the EMT to administer oxygen. Says here she has a history of heart problems and diabetes, reference her son in Cairns. Oh, here's—"

"What's he doing? Kurt asked. "Did you see that?"

Pacifica made a couple of jerky half-turns and back, as if the pilots were unsure what they wanted to do. "Whoa, girl," I said, sliding the Gulfstream into looser formation in case 1010 tried another abrupt maneuver.

"Something's up," Kurt said.

Pacifica rolled into a lazy turn to the left.

"Look at that, would ya," I said, my voice unable to conceal the joy.

As the 747 rolled out on a perfect heading to Nandi, Kurt said, "I'll be damned."

"Check the fuel, Kurt," I said. "Bridget..." She was gone.

"I'm checking," Bridget said from the console.

Kurt looked up from his calculator. "Fifteen hundred down."

"We'll have to land at Nandi," I said, relieved.

"Beats Hilo," he said.

"Okay, I've got it," Bridget said, plopping down on the jumpseat. "Mrs. Cranbrook woke up claiming to have fainted and says she's fine. The doctors said it was okay to continue to Brisbane with the option to land in Nandi if Mrs. Cranbrook should faint again. Monitor her and keep her on oxygen, they said."

I shook my head. "That's a relief." I eased the GV into a closer position as clouds approached.

"Thank you, Mrs. Cranbrook," Kurt said sarcastically.

We sat in silence for a long time. I lost myself in the folly of savoring another victory snatched from the jaws of defeat. How did Marcia manage to sleep through all that ruckus, I mused.

After awhile, Kurt looked at me and said, "There's enough fuel in the tanks to get us to within seventy-five miles of the island."

"We could swim in," I said.

Bridget twisted in her loose pajamas. "I'm staying with the money."

I looked at Kurt. "Are you thinking what I'm thinking?"

He grinned wide. "I think so."

"Okay, I give up, boys."

Kurt glanced at me as he turned to her. "When we split off from Pacifica, we'll shutdown one of the motors to save gas."

I shook my head and smiled at her.

"Then we avoid Nandi?" she said.

"Yes," Kurt said. "Let me check the numbers."

I focused on the underbelly of the whale, mesmerized by the flicker of her shiny skin each time the red beacon light flashed.

Kurt said, "With these winds," pointing to the INS, "and shutting a motor down for thirty minutes, we'll land with 1200 pounds."

I nodded my acceptance but realized there were too many ifs to make the final decision. The winds were a big if with five hours to go, and 1200 pounds gave us little room for error in finding the island.

"I'm going back to bed," Kurt said, looking at Bridget.

"Sure. I'll stay up with Duff," she said. "Let me get him some wet towels first."

"Okay."

"Thanks, Bridget," I said.

Kurt exited the cockpit saying, "Don't get lost again."

I laughed and said, "I'm in good hands now," glancing at Bridget. That slipped out before I thought about it, but I don't think Kurt took offense.

"Your eyes are so red and swollen," she said. "I don't know how you can see anything."

I slid back out to loose formation and rubbed my eyes one at a time.

With a warm towel, Bridget massaged gently around my eyes and wiped across my forehead. She took another wet towel and laid it across my shoulders after she rubbed them back to life. I took a rag and wiped my hands free of the stickiness and then cleaned off the controls with it. I felt rejuvenated in a hazy, temporary sort of way. Bridget slid into the copilot's seat.

"Kurt fell asleep up here, so I sent him back. I guess I shouldn't have done that," I said.

"No, you shouldn't be up here alone," she said in a motherly tone. She looked back. "He's dead to the world. Those sleepers are pretty comfortable." She winced. "Oh, I'm sorry."

"No problem," I said. "I'm feeling better now."

"I hate to say it, but you look like hell, Duff. I don't know how you're doing it."

That scared me. "I look that bad, huh?"

"Yes."

"I love your candor."

"I'm sorry—again."

To persevere over the extreme physical difficulty, I blocked the pain out of mind—a sort of mental novocaine. I had tricked my mind into overcoming my body. It was a game I enjoyed—how far could I push myself? "Well, I've found that the older I get, the more endurance I have, because I have greater self-discipline even though I have less physical strength," I said.

"I suppose I see what you're saying."

"You want to try it awhile?"

Bridget seemed taken aback. "Try what?"

"Flying."

"Yes, sure. I didn't want to ask. I was afraid of breaking your…well, concentration."

I explained how to do it. "Be very light and smooth on the controls," I said, "and move the throttles just a little bit to keep the airplane right where you want it."

She nodded.

I positioned the jet into a more relaxed formation. "Put your right hand on your yoke and put your left hand on the throttles and follow me along."

"Okay," she said. "What about the rudders?"

"Don't worry about the rudders. Keep your feet flat on the floor."

She squeaked out an "Okay."

I felt the tension she had in her hands through my controls. "You're tense. Loosen up. Roll your shoulders around and shake out your arms. Your fingers are too tight. Relax them." After about ten minutes, she loosened up, and I slowly released my yoke. My hands felt cramped from holding the same position all night. I kept my hands cupped near my yoke. Her flying was erratic.

"I don't know about this."

"You're doing fine. Relax and make smaller inputs. You'll get the hang of it." Her up and down started to dampen out but she sawed back and forth on the throttles, causing us to go up and back too much. "Here, I've got the throttles."

She released the throttles.

"You don't have to move the throttles as much." I showed her how to use them. I would put in a power setting and wait quite a long time before I had to make another adjustment, but that was because of my experience. "Do you want to try the throttles again?"

"No."

"I'll work the throttles then." I explained the technique of anticipation in formation, where you make changes before you see the need because you know you will need it. She said she understood what I meant, but I saw that she did not have the experience and judgment yet to anticipate. "Anticipation takes a while to get a feel for."

She nodded, but couldn't take her eyes off Pacifica.

"Sure you don't want to try the throttles again?"

"No," she said emphatically.

I didn't bother to explain that flying the engines was as important as flying the jet because doing one makes the other easier, provides leverage with both hands working, and gives the pilot control of all three dimensions. She was not ready to hear it, I decided. She did a pretty good job, but we had to be in too loose a position for her to feel comfortable, and as much instruction as I had to give her to keep her there, I decided to take over. The instruction exhausted me more than flying. Besides, if we encountered some weather, I was worried she would freeze up and cause us to loose sight of 1010. After discussing the transfer of control, I took the airplane and flew it back into position.

"Thanks for the formation lesson."

"No problem, you did great."

"Was that a good break for you?"

"Yes," I lied.

"I'm not leaving you alone up here again," Bridget said.

"Thanks. I enjoy your company." We talked for maybe an hour about lots of things, but she kept leading me into my history, especially my life with Claire. I told her a few things without telling her anything and it seemed to satisfy her. I knew she was smarter than that and I suspected Kurt had told her a few things, but I evaded the truth for the time being. We had been flying in clear weather, which made the conversation effortless, and besides, it helped keep me awake. Eventually, Kurt and Marcia woke up. Kurt came up first.

"Good, we're still on course," he said.

"Now, now. Bridget's been keeping me awake up here."

"That's my girl." He bent over, kissing her on the cheek.

"Feeling better?" she asked.

"Some."

"Good," Bridget said standing up, trading places with him. She hugged him around the shoulders and that seemed to buoy his spirits.

"How we doing?" Kurt asked with a yawn, waking to the wee hours of another day—a day soon to be ahead of the date on his watch.

"Good. I think I can go the distance," I said.

"Good, I'll take a close look at the fuel." He looked at me a second time and said, "Are you sure you're okay?"

"I know Bridget told me how bad I look. I feel like I'm in the last few miles of a triathlon—the surreal phase where you just keep going," I said seriously. "You know what I mean?"

"Yeah, okay." He studied the flight plan and the INS. "Three and a half hours to go."

"Is that all?" I said.

"No problem getting to Nandi," he said. "The island looks iffy. Lets see…with these winds, we'll land on the island with 1100 pounds."

"That's a hundred pounds lower than before," Bridget said.

"I checked it twice," Kurt said.

"Is it based on flying the last hour on the deck as we planned?" I asked.

"Yes, but if we miss it we're screwed," he said. "We'll run out of gas trying to find it. It's not easy to see, especially when it's hazy."

"We'll need to get a good update on the INS over Fiji," I said. "It's been tight so far compared to Pacifica's position reports."

"Good," Kurt said. "If we fly over a good geographical reference, I'll make an update; otherwise, we'll have to take what we got and plan to fly a little higher to make sure we find it the first time around."

"Sounds good," I said.

"There's lots of islands out there to get an update from," Bridget said looking over the maps. "That shouldn't be a problem, should it?"

"No, but we've got to be careful who we fly over," Kurt said. "Don't want to blow it now."

"Here's a good one, Apia. Are we flying over Apia?"

"Let me see your map."

She handed it to him.

Kurt compared the coordinates on the map with the coordinates of the checkpoints in the INS. "Yep, here it is. Apia looks good for an update." He handed the map back to Bridget.

"Apia's good," I said. "It's isolated enough. I've flown over it on the 747 lots of times."

Kurt toggled up the INS. "An hour and eight minutes to Apia," he said looking at me then back at Bridget.

"My God, it's been a long night," I said.

Marcia greeted us with food. We ate sandwiches and fruit, and I drank more water.

"Where are we?" Marcia asked.

"Two hours from Nandi," Kurt answered. "That's in Fiji."

"I've been to Nandi," she said.

"Really," Kurt said.

Marcia poured water on a towel and began wiping me down. It felt real good. I felt like a boxer about to be sent in for the last round.

"I spent a day there when I was flying international. We had to divert there because Sydney fogged in," she said. "It's a pretty place."

"As long as we don't land there this morning, I'll be happy," Bridget said.

"We're gonna make it, aren't we Duff?" Marcia said confidently and sounding in better spirits than before she went to bed.

"We're gonna make it," I said.

"Bridget, please check the console to see if there are any updates on our Mrs. Cranbrook," I said.

"No problem." She retrieved all the messages between Pacifica headquarters and flight 1010. After a minute or so she said, "Says here, Mrs. Cranbrook's condition has stabilized and it looks like 1010 is planning to fly all the way to Brisbane."

"Who's Mrs. Cranbrook?" Marcia asked.

We brought Marcia up to speed on the medical emergency and the possibility that Pacifica might have to divert into Nandi (didn't really matter at that point because we were to fly from Nandi to the island without cover anyway).

"Sounds like a close call," she said.

"It was closer than you know," Kurt said. "And still is."

I chuckled, then briefed her on our plan to shut one of the engines down after we split from 1010.

She asked me, "Is that a good idea?"

"It's the best option we have," I said.

"Flight 1010's estimating Brisbane on time now and they're up two thousand pounds," Bridget said as she pulled up the most recent message.

"That's why they slowed to Mach .82," I said.

"That helps our fuel situation, doesn't it?" Bridget asked.

"Yes," Kurt said, "it will and has. We'd have to land in Nandi if they'd kept the speed they started with."

"Or Hilo," I said.

"Right," he said.

"I can't believe we're rich in just one night," Marcia said with girlish excitement.

"Two days when we cross the international dateline," Kurt said. He set his watch.

"We'll cross it just after Apia," Bridget said, pointing to her map.

"That's right," Marcia said. "You've lost *two* nights of sleep, Duff."

"Three actually; feels like a month."

"Duff, are you sure you're going to give me eight million dollars just for being here?" Marcia asked.

"I'm buying your anonymity. You deserve more," I said.

"I wish we could keep a joint account, Duff. I don't feel comfortable with that much money."

"You'll get used to it real fast," Kurt said. "I've never known a woman who didn't know what to do with money."

"Marcia," I said, "you'll be fine. Don't sweat it." The idea of not having to support another human ever again had taken strong root in my mind, and I liked it. It had been only a few hours but that door—revolving for years—was now shut solid, sealed off like a vault in a graveyard of close secrets. "I'll help you find a financial planner."

"Let's say everything works out and we each get eight million," Bridget said with a pause, which let me know she understood the obstacles awaiting us. "We get the money but it doesn't make us happy or it makes us less happy than we were before, then what do we do?"

"It's too late for that. We've been over this before," Kurt said.

"I never thought of that," Marcia said. "Can't turn back, that's all I know."

"I'm perfectly serious," Bridget said. "I'm playing the devil's advocate here. What's going to happen?"

"I don't know. Might lead to more crime, maybe a life of crime," I said to appease her.

"Then it's worth a hell of a lot more than eight million," she said.

"Don't look at me," Marcia said. She handed me another bottle of water. "I never think that way."

For the first time, I feared Bridget and Marcia were incompatible.

"If it leads to more crime then the money's not worth anything because you won't be able to relax," Kurt said. "Relaxation, that's what this is all about for me."

"Without complete anonymity, we'll never relax, 'cause the Feds will hound us forever," I said. "We'll be on the lam till the end."

Kurt smiled as if I had given him a cue. "I've got anonymity for you. It's in my suitcase. Multiple aliases with supporting documents—birth certificates, passports, visas. You name it, it's all there just waiting for you…to assume."

"That's not anonymity, that's schizophrenia," Bridget said.

"I wish you wouldn't make light of my condition," I said. There seemed to be some truth to it the way I had faded in and out of coherence.

Everyone laughed.

"Anonymity or not, all I want out of this is to be with you, Duff," Marcia said. "That's all. Forget the money. I'd live in a shack on New Guinea if it meant being with Duff."

"That's sweet, Marcia," I said, concentrating more on formation because a ridge of clouds—impregnated at intervals by the gauzy red beacon flashes, weaving a foggy trail of blinking light—whisked across the windscreen.

"You need more than love," Bridget said.

Kurt looked back at Marcia and said, "I'd get along just fine in the poorhouse with Marcia's brand of love."

"Thanks, Kurt. At least somebody understands me."

"I mean that," he said, smiling at her.

"I'll love you, Kurt, just give me your cut," Bridget said gravely.

"You loved me when I was poor," Kurt said. "I'm not worried about you, Bridget. You're a big talker."

The cockpit was silent once more. I waited for someone to say something—anything, but I could not talk. My eyes were padlocked on Pacifica because the clouds had gotten thicker, and all I saw of the 747 was the faint sweeps of the flashing red light. I tucked in real close—less than three feet away—and held her steadily. I became disoriented staring at the light and then waiting in darkness—for what seemed an eternity—between flashes. I didn't want to go lost wingman, because it meant losing our escort for good. I hung in during the periods of darkness, counting to myself, "One potato, two potato," (three potato meant breaking it off) and then he would obscurely reappear for a second—until all the lingering light faded away, and I would have to start the cycle over again. I could have sworn we were flying upside down. I had no idea how long it would last, but I could not think about being tired.

"I'm going back to bed," Bridget said. "I think Duff has plenty of company now."

"Don't be sore, Bridget," Kurt said. "It's nothing personal. We were talking…philosophically."

Mark A. Putch

I heard nothing out of Bridget.

"I'm sorry, Kurt," Marcia said.

"It's not your fault," Kurt said. Out of the corner of my eye, I saw a hand touch his shoulder.

"How are you doing, Duff?" Marcia asked.

I managed to mumble, "I'm working like a dog." I don't believe she ever realized how hard I worked to keep from losing our leader. None of that rotten conversation would have mattered if I had, I remember thinking. I felt fortunate to have Marcia—a real gem, I marveled.

Marcia went back to the console as she said, "I guess it's time I work the radios."

A long few minutes went by with nobody saying anything. Kurt knew how hard I had been working, but the clouds eventually seemed thinner and the air

PACIFIC PASSAGES

smoothed out. I relaxed some, flying the Gulfstream to a looser position. Strangely, I'd adjusted to the demands placed on my flying, and, oddly enough, enjoyed the higher workload; it was the times of boredom when I would get into trouble.

"Kurt," Marcia called. "I just realized I don't know how to work this thing."

"I'll be right back," he said. "Will you be okay up here alone for a few minutes, Duff? Marcia needs a little help."

"Sure, I'll be fine. Can you bring me a water before you and Marcia get busy?"

He set the bottle in a cup holder next to the throttle console. I thanked him.

"No sweat," he said. "Sure you're okay?"

"I'm feeling much better. Go help Marcia."

Mark A. Putch

I left the water there until the weather broke up. Later, when things settled down, I peed in the empty bottle and placed it at the end of the row of bottles I had lined up along the floor on my left. I felt embarrassed, so I didn't ask anyone to get rid of them for me (in a way I couldn't explain, they were like trophies of the night, and I wondered if I had peed to drink or drank to pee—it helped pass the time, you see?).

The parade of yellow bottles reminded me of all those urine tests I had taken over the years. I had never been comfortable with that either—too intimate. Amazing how nurses and technicians handled the specimens as if they were carrying around a cup of tea. It seems people get used to whatever they work with: doctors with death, preachers with sinners, lawyers with criminals, judges with punishment—capital punishment, even soldiers with killing, and trash collectors with garbage, of all things.

It did not take long before I was feeling exhausted again. The trip was just too long for one pilot, and I had way too much time on my hands—which felt cramped, numb and desensitized.

There I went again, feeling as if I had been swimming upstream against black-hole gravity, tumbling out of control into the tarred abyss of the night—free-falling toward black, sticky guilt: the blood of a cop on my hands, literally. I tried to block the shooting from my mind like a bad hangover—I am good at forgetting hangovers, but the more I denied it, the more it came to roost on Claire's murder. Murder: All of a sudden, here I was—a dissenter—painfully tallying the score.

Mark A. Putch

Vietnam didn't count, did it? That was war, and killing was the rule. The Army taught me how to kill, but they did not teach me the difference of not killing. We were so gung-ho back them. "Kill anything that moves," they would say. Killing preserves a nation or creates one, but killing in a nation is murder—a subtle distinction I had missed along the way. I had committed capital murder in a tragedy bearing less malignance and premeditation than a national consciousness waging war in sanctioned killing, but I was still the criminal, a criminal of the most despised brand—a cop killer.

Vietnam made me a proud and brave warrior—not always appreciated back then—with a clear conscience, but within a few short hours I had gone from war hero to robber, felon and murderer. I thought about it for a few minutes, fashioning a strategy of denial, but stumbled over its clumsy, up-to-date design. Denial ruled deeply, below the conscious level, embedded in sealed stores and discarded from memory like buried radiation. Therein lay the pinch. Into the stream of consciousness flowed water so foul, seeped from wellsprings defiled. Despite my great struggles to seal the effluvial valve, the leak would not be dammed.

Why did I have to drown in guilt all of a sudden? Hadn't I been a *true* murderer for a long time, longer in years—twice as long—than the hours of one hellish night? No, hogwash: the ramblings of a delirious fool. I could not do it. How could I stare into the bright lights of those cameras and say the things I said with that much sincerity if I had done it? Impossible, I'm too honest—if you can call being a bad liar honest.

How could I lie with a crystal-clear conscience? If I had killed her, my eyes and body would have given it away. No, I am innocent; I have to be. I proved it, *did I not?*

Reasonable doubt is proof enough to console the conscience, is it not? It worked for me. If it is legal, is it not worthy and right? We are a people of law, they said. Liberated guilt is liberation for an advanced society, and we are an enlightened people—cut loose from the medieval shackles of shame.

Damn it, the thunder boomed incessantly in Atlanta that sultry summer night. Every horizon was lit up with thunderheads—mountainous, billowy, gray-white statues—weaving themselves into the earth's fabric with crackling veins of lightning and patch-quilted sheets of rain that smashed against the ground in diagonal assaults. Plates of rain splashed down into flooded puddles and drummed their fury against rooftops—wave after wave—all night long.

She got home late, having flown in from somewhere in Canada—Calgary, I think it was—carrying breast milk for our daughter in a brown paper bag.

We had a son, too. He was twelve when it happened, and he ended up—as did my daughter—living with his grandparents (Claire's parents) in Boulder; that is, until the acquittal and I won legal custody of him. The courts would not give me custody of Sara, my daughter. They said she was too young and in better hands with her grandparents. I had little contact with her because her grandparents fought me tooth and nail, poisoning her mind against me. I didn't even know where Sara lived; she is grown now and I would not recognize her if she were standing right here.

My son got hooked up with a bunch of zealous Christian types, and they made him into a missionary. He said the only way he could survive the tragedy of his mother was to give it all to Jesus. He tried to sell me on that stuff, and I told him flat out to forget it, but I am happy for him if that is what he needed.

He never gave me much trouble growing up. Well, there was that time when he was a teenager and he pulled a gun on me and threatened to kill me, same as I had killed his mother, he said. He had been drinking—I smelled it—and was high on something. I calmly talked some sense into him, telling him he would not prove anything by killing me. We had a real good talk—I was sitting there calmly and he was shaking, including the gun in his hand until it finally fell to the floor and he wrapped himself in my arms sobbing. It was not long after that when he started going to church.

I am glad he found peace in religion, because if he did not have faith, he would never have accepted me as his father—that much, I understood. I am happy for Robbie; he is a good kid.

The cops believed she had been murdered in the house late that night, but I did not know. The last people to see her were her crewmembers when she left the airport that night. It all came out in the investigation, and I talked to them.

They parted shaking hands. She had flown with a couple of ex-fighter pilots with an established hierarchy too ingrained to conceal and too proud to accept as peers those pilots of lesser aviation backgrounds—civilian backgrounds, particularly if they were women. Despite their hard-boiled notions of black and white, of right and wrong, of fighter pilot and non-fighter pilot, of military trained and civilian trained, of the crushing, inexplicable blows to their simplified approach to life that had been socially structured and organized like a neatly stacked bookshelf of leather bound *subject books*, despite this—the assault on their faded traditions—they shook her hand with respect and chivalry and said they enjoyed flying with her. (Women in the cockpit had changed everything these men ever knew about the career, and they just couldn't deal with it. Claire, being their captain, only compounded their chagrin.) Their wives provided solid alibis to investigators.

The cops said she had been beaten over the head with a blunt instrument. I did not remember having any baseball bats in the house, because I never played baseball and my son didn't like sports. They said whoever beat her—they believed I did—beat the hell out of her and was a brutal and violent individual, and it had taken a strong man to inflict that much damage on a person.

Eldon swore to them that I wasn't home, and he had the hotel receipts and telephone charges to prove it. Eldon's wife said—under oath—he was with her when it happened. I had a business trip scheduled, and Eldon usually went with me. He had been my mechanic and I never flew the King Air out of town without him, but I know he was there.

Eldon could fly too, but he didn't have a license because he couldn't pass the written test. He could turn a wrench though, and I think he had a license for it. He said he did, although I never saw it—being afraid to ask. The Marines trained him. They had taught him how to pass the test, he said. Oh yes, Eldon was good mechanic; he could fix things.

We had never canceled a parachute jamboree for mechanical reasons because Eldon kept the airplane in excellent condition. Our customers could rely on us to show up. We would fly around the country charging a flat fee for unlimited jumps. Modern-day barnstorming, that is what it was. It would attract the same type of person that would go to those all-you-can-eat country buffets. Trough feeding, I called it, a distinctly American indulgence that we learned to exploit. We charged them each a couple hundred dollars for the day and they would get up to ten jumps—a lot of jumps for one day. We would pack up to fourteen jumpers in the plane and make a little bit of money doing something we absolutely loved. When we started the business Claire got a license plate that read "OH CHUTE."

That was the weekend we went to Louisville. Lots of jumpers showed up on Friday and Saturday. My son flew with me on many of those flights but that really upset Claire. She reported me to the FAA because passengers were not allowed on jump flights.

Robbie loved being in the air. I taught him how to fly before he could drive a car. He flies for the mission now. He was a natural pilot and I had dreams of his joining the airlines someday, but he said he preferred flying for the mission. "It's very rewarding," he had said. "I wouldn't trade places with you, Dad." I did not understand what he meant at first.

Mark A. Putch

The FAA thing really pissed me off. I wanted to strangle her. She wanted to destroy me, peeling away the internal onion of my soul one torturous layer at a time. With her every flaying attack, my heart ached a little more, but getting my license suspended was the last scalping I would take. I couldn't take it anymore. My heart still aches when I think about it. She stabbed at everything I had loved, seeing it as competition for her attention. I always felt she had been jealous of my success because I was a go-getter, adventuring through life while she preferred an anchoring approach, secured to the dry dock (excuse the pun, but it was very dry to me) of closed domestic circles.

In that way, we were opposites. While I accumulated wealth, she gave generously—recklessly—to charity. My idea of a vacation was scuba diving in the Cayman Islands while hers was exploring the Holy Land of Jerusalem. I spent Sundays working and flying. She spent them glued to a pew and serving up fried chicken at community picnics. If I envisioned having couples over for dinner, she saw them participating in a home bible study.

My recreation was golf or a workout at the fitness center, and hers was browsing the clearance racks at Penny's. My idea of a good layover was nineteen hours in Boston or Vancouver, B.C., and hers was in Des Moines with a book and a bubble bath. We were never together, I recalled. The continual bickering, and acrimony of clashing interests, was just too painful for me.

I could not honestly explain how we ended up being married. The closest thing to honesty is that she was a pilot and I saw an opportunity to make lots of combined income—you know how much money meant to me. Why?—I still can't tell you. I realize that tragedy in life is already having something I'm searching for and not knowing it. That is a foolish reason to get married, but if I could kill her, I could easily marry her for money. *What! What did you mean, you didn't kill her—remember.* I had to remind myself. *You're an evil bastard.*

I don't want to go there, but as long as I'm glued to the mother ship I have to go where she takes me. The mother ship will lead not into temptation and despair but deliver me to the Promised Land.

Everything was going fine after the murder. The grand jury had convened but seemed at an impasse; they lacked certain vigor—compelling evidence had eluded them—until Beverly spoiled it. I had been sleeping with her for about a year before the murder when Claire caught us in the marital bed. Beverly had been the live-in nanny. We could not raise two kids on airline schedules—both of us captains—without a nanny. Beverly had been a poor choice though because she was attractive and cunning. I fell for her and she played the role like a cardsharp, dealing the dependable cards of our marital problems from her too-familiar deck. My wounds laid the foundation for entanglement.

At first—when I found out how heavily she drank—I tried to fire her, but Claire balked. Claire wanted to help her out. I requested that Beverly insulate the kids from her boozing and she did, for the most part, but before long I found myself enjoying her company when Claire was away on flying trips. One thing led to the other and the rest was history.

I explained to Claire after she caught us that Beverly had filled the vacuum of rejection I had felt after our daughter was born. Claire directed all her attention to Sara, neglecting me. Claire and I had not had sex in a year. "I just don't feel like it," she'd say. "You're a real turn off."

I tried to reason with her, explaining it was only natural that I would be attracted to Beverly. She did not buy it at all and never forgave me. Claire fired Beverly the next day.

When I would not marry Beverly after the murder—that would look too suspicious to the grand jury—she went to the police and told them I murdered Claire. Next thing I know, I was in the slammer. My lawyer posted bail and worked up a fine defense by branding Beverly as the spurned mistress with a long history of drug and alcohol abuse and a wretched history of failed relationships (interestingly, most of it was true). She had several ex-husbands and an extensive rap sheet of various misdemeanors related to alcohol use.

She broke down on the stand when Terrance cross-examined her. He hacked away at her credibility with one piercing question after the other. I felt sorry for her—after the acquittal—because I knew she loved me and her life had been so miserable, but, unfortunately, she tried to cross a dangerous intersection in the road of life and got squashed. She entered an alcohol rehabilitation program after the trial, and I have not heard from her since.

The trial was no walk in the park, though. It didn't help my case when they brought out Claire's medical records that had documented two trips to the hospital to treat cuts and bruises to her face and arms. Everybody knew we had some violent fights, especially the time she put a steak knife to my balls. (She had been slicing cheese in the Jacuzzi to go with our wine.) I can't believe she survived that beating. My reaction—and that is all it was, instinct—had been to beat her about the face and head with the palm of my hand. She looked bad for a long time after that.

She tried to hide our fights, making up stories of car wrecks and bike spills. Everybody saw right through her lies. I think she felt too guilty to admit the truth—before she filed for divorce and we were still trying to work things out. I hate that I lost my temper with her a few times. I still feel guilty about it. It had been wrong and my reputation was at risk, so I quit doing it—*until I could wrap it all up for good.* Damn, that echoed in my mind. *Now stop that.*

The mother ship sailed into the inferno of hell, impelled by the floggings of a fearless galley-master, I saw, lashing the six weary rowers through smoky, hell-bent gates. The last batch of clouds thinned out and finally became easier to see through, and staying tucked next to the 747 took less effort this time.

Ungluing my cramped right hand from the throttle quadrant, I rubbed the burn from my eyes one at a time and massaged around the temples. My body filled the chair like an overflowing sack of flour, limp and heavy. Over the noise of wind smashing against the windscreen, constant, annoying, fatiguing, I heard the murmuring voices of Kurt and Marcia.

Since we were going to shut the right engine down after splitting from Pacifica, I decided on my own—

not wanting to bother Kurt and Marcia—to feed both engines with the fuel in the right wing. That way, I figured, when we would be running just on the left engine, I would feed it directly from the left wing tank. It would save us the worry of cross-feeding fuel between both wings to feed the left engine. Preemptive planning was all I was doing, and it sounded like a good idea at the time. If nothing else, it took my mind off Claire for awhile.

Claire had a way of taking me right up to the edge, my toes dangling over the cliff of sanity. Once, she donated $50,000 to the church in a lump sum—to make up for lost time. She had not been tithing and the guilt caught up to her. That ranked up there with her notifying the FAA in her quest to elicit my anger. Her impulsiveness drove me crazy; her willingness to run to the charity of any cause, I never understood. Claire was the quintessential buyer that telemarketing scoundrels and junk mail solicitors targeted. She lacked the certain hard, cold instinct of survivors: the genetic code for selection. She deserved death for a lack of sophistication in a survivalist world, I rationalized. God, what am I saying? *Make it stop! Please, God!*

Don't get me wrong. Every time my mind succumbed to the need of rationalizing Claire's death, I would remind myself that we were in love once upon a time. We had a great time before she lost herself with church and religion. We made passionate love between the satin sheets of fine hotels all around the world. She was my copilot then.

We took exotic trips, tucking ourselves away in intimate seclusion: *soft, hot flesh shining under sun and sultry star, entangled silken thigh on soft bed of sand, sweet and sticky the dewdrops of hummingbird nectar—our passions elicited. Butlers bow curtsy of palm branch and breeze, seagulls trill songs, air pierced of virginal brine, driftwood and mangrove still and all. Seawater lapping kisses at our feet. Seaside cliffs—waves pound against faltering legs—mounting rapturous gardens of lush plateaus.*

I wanted to be a lover, but the stress of harsh words and routine—the day-in-and-day-out grind and expectation—of married life exacted a high toll on love. Even after marriage things were good for awhile—until religion came home to roost on guilt. We had frolicked in a sea of sin until the biblical life preserver came floating by like a temptress. The appeal overcame Claire—she lived but the fun died.

She believed the careless rhetoric—the coin-sloppy words—of preachers. I told her that the preacher's job was to give people a moral compass and lead their congregations on spiritual matters and that the people of their flocks were guilty of everything—but they didn't change. They would listen and nod—drool streaming from the cusp of their mouths, they would profess to believe far-fetched stories of faith, and they would live an illusion of the impossible, but they would never change because they are humans with inalienable instincts that have allowed the race to survive for thousands of years. All religion could hope to do was discourage the most heinous human behavior, and thus had some practical value. Concede the floodwaters of humanity and let's get on with it, I said to her.

As far as I was concerned, Western Christianity would make a nice elective course in college one day, much the same as Greek mythology. Claire could not even fathom it; she was hell-bent for God. I did not have anything against God, but I expected her to apply a little moderation and common sense.

She had believed everything the preacher said, especially the hogwash about premarital sex. From it, she extrapolated a doomed marriage. It was the unpardonable curse on our marriage, she said. I said, "Bullshit," but she didn't listen to me.

I had already lost her to the preacher, who had praised her as "a generous and kind creature of God's kingdom" when they interviewed him on the TV the day after the murder. Claire was a victim of human guilt stoked to a high pitch by the religious zealotry.

"Hypocrisy is a true antidote," I suggested she consider, but she did not understand it in the practical sense. Guilt held her in an emotional trap. The Christians used a cheap trick to ensnare her, but it was the usual tactic: a front for the rancorous control that brand of Christians craved. Guilt destroyed her self-image because she had made all the classic mistakes of the past: alcohol, drugs, and sex, all the common sins of the seventies.

She had been married before, and they had taught her that divorce was a sin, too. By God, they had never given her any slack. Funny how she would rationalize some things. She had some twisted logic about the divorce—something he did, adultery, maybe?—which let her shed some weighty guilt in the quicksand. Then at other times, nothing mattered, she would carry the full load around her neck, and I figured the weight of it all toppled over on itself. Conscience was a tricky thing to manage; perhaps only the subconscious mind can manage the balance.

When Claire started reading her Bible in the cockpit—often aloud, trying to convert her fellow crewmembers—she pissed a lot of people off. Even the Christians she flew with dreaded her sermons. She used her position as a bully pulpit and nobody liked it; I know, they all told me. She got a bad reputation as a religious fanatic.

If she had made the conversion without going off the deep end, it would have been okay. I did get some enjoyment out of church—the people were mostly sincere, but when church won out over me, I resented it. Nothing I said or did was good enough; she constantly tied me to sinister motives and evildoing.

"I'm married to Satan," she would say. "I can't sleep with Satan."

Her exorcist was divorce, a relief to me. She justified it with her faith, because I had been the evil spirit that haunted her—another twisted rationalization. Did Christianity make exception for divorce from the spiritual enemy himself? Surely, she must have thought so.

Claire did not leave the exorcism to the spiritual realm; she expected financial assurances far and above the norm, threatening to quit flying to raise the kids in the crusade to stick it to me for exorbitant alimony and child support. She struck at my soul, demanding everything. When it came to my money, I decided to fight—fight hard, with every intention of winning.

I felt woozy, in and out of the clouds, hot flashes of madness sweeping across my twisted face, gummed with sweat and grime. Every flash of red light coming from 1010's wobbly form—obscured fitfully with the whisking paint of cloud and my own shadowy coherence—became more nauseating and surreal. *All I want is to sleep. Welcome, sleep! Sweet sleep! Please—*

I won all right, but at what cost—at what self-denying cost: murder! Was I a murder?—a three-time murderer and a thief. *No, it's not true! Eldon said so.* Everything was taken care of, he said, just like the first time—when Claire's chute didn't open. She tumbled helplessly toward the earth with nothing more than a streamer, and then—seconds before impact—the reserve chute opened. That was at the Ocala jamboree. "Everything's taken care of," he had said. I thought he meant the airplane was ready to fly. He was a good mechanic: the best I ever knew.

After that she got the "OH CHUTE" license plate. Amazingly, she didn't seem mad or scared but she never jumped again, even after promising me she would when I said it would be best to get back up there, just the way I told Kurt to get back in the saddle, but he didn't listen, either. If he had I would not have gotten so damn tired and would not have had to follow the mother ship through places I did not want to go.

My absolute exhaustion was a sort of insanity, but I often wondered if I could be insane if I knew I was insane. *Anything can be insane; it's all insane.* I mean—it's weird—the sanity of human insanity. Terrance taught me about it in case we needed it for the trial. Luckily we didn't. I couldn't see admitting to being insane, even if it were temporary. It scared me that it might be true. *I need it.* Insanity would have shielded my guilt. I decided insanity was hypocrisy for guilt, or was it guilt the hypocrisy of sanity?—I forgot.

I'm insane! I flew like a Thunderbird pilot though. That's it, I was an insane Thunderbird pilot. It made things more fun. *I'm insane! I'm insane! I'm a murdering madman, flying like a Thunderbird. What a shame—*

The cops found her in a burning van at daybreak in an Alabama cornfield off I-20—near the Georgia line. The coroner said she had been beaten to death twenty-four hours earlier. All the paint on the license plate had been burned off and all you could see was the raised letters of "OH CHUTE." The tires had melted off the rims and the windows had shattered into a million smoke-stained pieces. The remains of her charred carcass lay across the rear seat, and that was the first clue that she had died before being placed in the van—a scheme to destroy evidence according to the district attorney. The coroner testified that cracks in the skull are what killed her, and not the fire. How they had known it was twenty-four hours earlier that she breathed her last breath—in my merciless hands, as they put it—I never understood and neither did the jury. *Thank God for the jury, right Eldon? Right on—*

I watched the film clips later—Terrance got them from the TV stations—about my having fled for a week with the kids in the King Air. We, Eldon and I, calculated the timeline the way Hollywood makes cartoons—very carefully, one frame at a time. Eldon was such a good mechanic; he could fix anything. I owe it all to him, but I would hate for our paths to cross again. I confirmed my admiration and disdain for him in one sentence, I mused. I wish I could have remembered that week a little better. Maybe, then I would able to put the whole thing behind me. On second thought, I am glad I didn't. Since I had survived—thrived—in a defensive existence, memory barriers seemed to have a purpose.

Of course, I had plenty of motives: costly divorce with my name being dragged through the streets. I lusted after the insurance money to expand my business. Claire humiliated me with heart-piercing rejection for the surrogate husband of religion. I had a mistress who became increasingly hostile toward Claire as her attacks mounted. I was a white male control freak about to lose everything. Why wouldn't I kill her? I could solve all my problems rather conveniently—I would not even have a divorce on my record. I would award myself with closure, avoiding every hated compromise.

When Beverly testified to the grand jury that I told her I had to kill Claire two days prior to the murder, over the Labor Day weekend, the jury believed her—at first. I remembered saying it, but I don't remember killing her—exactly.

I had some burns on my hands and arms that caused a sensation. The prosecutor's office ordered me to take a physical exam to document them as evidence. Eldon and I had worked on one of the King Air's motors that weekend. It caught on fire, and that is how I had gotten those burns. Eldon testified about it and had the evidence to show it. The cops thought they had something when they raided my house and confiscated a jar of skin lightener, three tubes of ointment and three boxes of nonstick pads. The media made such a heyday out of it, everyone knew for sure that I would fry.

The lawyers had decided that I pay thirty-five percent of my gross income to Claire until the kids reached twenty-three years old. I was scheduled to sign the settlement on Tuesday—the first business day following the Labor Day weekend. I did not like it one bit, but what choice did I have at that point? The agreement terms rankled me until I thoroughly despised it. The numbers ran through my mind—over and over—like a flood of toxic sludge: forty-five percent to taxes and thirty-five percent to Claire. Devastation! I hated it. I had worked too hard in my life to cheapen my labor—already mortgaged too high—when Claire made as much as I did. I would not work for twenty-percent, no way. Where is the relief? I had asked. I hated the system with a passion. I'd do anything—*would I?*—to escape a court-decreed restriction upon my freedom. That weekend, I obsessed over the state of financial slavery I was about to enter into. Here I was making a bundle of jack on paper and having to live like a pauper.

She wanted me bankrupt; she hated the skydiving business and would do anything to attack it. She said, "Bankruptcy will bring you closer to God." I wanted to scream at the bitch. The way I saw it, the business was my only hope to recover financially because I controlled the books. I could not shelter anything from Coastal—the W-2 was nearly public property. It might have worked out with the business, but when the FAA slapped the sixty-day suspension on my license, I was livid and truly devastated.

Mark A. Putch

When they indicted me for murder, my father-in-law got custody of the kids and filed a twenty-million-dollar wrongful death lawsuit against me. I was sunk. My wife was dead, kids gone, Coastal bankrupt, Eldon crashed the King Air and Beverly disappeared. Did I feel closer to God, you ask? Hell no, I was desperate. I killed her—in one way or the other, and she destroyed my well-being. Nobody won; we both lost. I did get Robbie back, and I'm thankful I got to raise him. I wish it had been different with Sara. Benson did not get twenty million, but a good chunk of Claire's insurance money, the balance going to settle lawsuits from Eldon crashing the King Air. I had some equity in the house in Atlanta and all of that I managed to salvage, it going into the house Janelle now owns in

California. I lost it all—except one very good friend who stuck with me all the way, thank God.

Kurt testified for me at the murder and the civil trials. The juries loved him. He was an Air Force Academy graduate, tall, handsome, baby-faced, and honest as Abe Lincoln. He rescued me from the death spiral when he got me hired at Pacifica. I would never betray Kurt, I thought, and if I did it would be the worst case of double-dealing since Alger Hiss and Whittaker Chambers. How could I think of it? *I'm a very bad person. I'm unworthy.*

And the lawyers, suffice it to say they cost me a bundle. I didn't mind paying for Robbie's college education but when Terrance enrolled his son at Yale Law School and began mentioning it while we were taking depositions and planning for trial, I wasn't sure there wouldn't be another murder. By the time every detail of my life cycled through the billing department of Terrance's firm, I couldn't wait for the trial to end. The legal bills for the divorce mounted just as high.

Claire used adultery as grounds for divorce because biblical law allowed divorce for adultery: Claire's graceful exit. "I can divorce you and keep my church membership. I'm glad I kept Beverly on," she had said. I told her, "And you think I'm the devil." I don't think guilt figured in when it came to divorcing me. She had some strange inconsistencies I could not figure out.

I had to kill her! I had to kill her! I just had to kill her! She must die! Die now, please God, die now! It's not as hard as it looks. Eldon, make it stop. You can fix it. You're the mechanic. Please Eldon, make it stop! Eldon, fix it!

The burning, as gruesome as it sounded, was nothing more than a way to dispose of the body—like a cremation. It was cold and stiff and lifeless by then. I had no feelings for it. I only thought about getting rid of it. That is the one thing I could have done better, but it is always the biggest problem—what to do with the body?

The first blow is hard because they are alive. We forget about what we are doing and just do it quickly— the way we drop bombs on people. We can't think about who we are killing. We don't think about sons and daughters and mothers and fathers, we think of them as the same ruthless enemy they think we are. We think about doing it quickly and well—before they kill us. I had to kill her before she killed me; that's what it was. She tried to kill me slowly, one court decree at a time. So I had to kill her right. I hit her in her sleep across the head with a bat and I did it so well she was dead by the first thump. I hit her some more but it was like whacking a carcass of beef. It was wasted effort. The damage was done. *No, I didn't do it. Eldon, I did not do it. I am not the trigger-man, am I?* Nobody knew.

Everything was calculated with military precision. All I had to do was follow the steps of the timeline—the flowchart—just as Eldon instructed. Getting away with murder was developing the right timeline, Eldon said. Old Eldon, where the hell was he now? I hope he is doing fine fixing things. He was a real mechanic. *Come on, Eldon, can you fix it? You hit her, didn't you? You have all the tools, don't you? You know all the tricks, you—*

Marcia entered the cockpit, plopping down in the jumpseat. "My God, Duff, what's wrong? You're soaked."

I looked at her.

"And your eyes look like they're swollen shut."

Tears dribbled down my cheeks.

"You've got blood in the wrinkles of your face," she said.

I glanced at my forearms. In the creases of skin were trails of blood that looked like runny eyeliner. The controls of the airplane sweated blood. I felt as if I were swimming in blood. I glanced back to Marcia. "I'm just thinking about everything, that's all."

She hugged me as best she could. I put the airplane in a looser formation position. We were out of the clouds and, as well as I could tell in the darkness, it appeared clear ahead. The moon had set and the ocean looked like a tar pit. I couldn't see any stars from my position. I felt like we were flying through a time zone that didn't exist.

"I'm sorry," Marcia said. "I know you're under a great deal of pressure. It's been a hard night—or lifetime, I don't know which one. One life ends, another begins—overnight. We're grieving over our past life. I'm forgetting the past right here and now. The future's all that matters.... We have no other choice."

I unfurled my fingers from the throttles and placed my arm around her waist. She knelt next to me, and I ran my hand up her back, resting my arm on her shoulder. We drifted away from Pacifica. I did nothing to correct the problem for awhile—until we were about a half-mile behind. I needed the break and

Marcia made me feel good. I savored the moment. Marcia looked at me inquisitively, but didn't say anything. Eventually, I pushed the power up and closed in on Pacifica. "I'm glad you're in my future."

"It's a bright future."

"A bright future it shall be. A toast to a bright future."

"Here, here."

Marcia got some more towels and rubbed me down, cleaning off the blood and massaging my shoulders back to life. The cramps went away for awhile and I began to feel refreshed, but my eyes were so tired. I appreciated the temporary fix, but mostly I was happy that Marcia was back to her normal self.

Kurt moved into the copilot's seat. "Fiji, I assume?" He pointed.

"Yes," I said. "That's Suva. Nandi's on the far side. That's the island of Vanua Levu over there to the right." I pointed across the cockpit.

"It's beautiful," Marcia said, leaning forward.

"Yes, it is," Kurt said, looking in the distance at the lights of Suva in the early morning darkness. "Looks beautiful down there."

"It's beautiful, all right," I said, feeling a resurgence of confidence that I'd be able to do the distance.

"Did we pass Apia already?" Marcia asked.

I nodded. "Bout an hour ago." Oddly, I could not recall seeing it. Must have been in the clouds. We talked about getting the update to the INS over Nandi as we had missed Apia.

Kurt turned to Marcia. "Would you get Bridget up, please?"

Marcia woke Bridget then came back up while Kurt studied the flight plan, checking it against the INS and the map. "What's up with the fuel, Duff? We've got a 1500 pound imbalance."

I explained to him about packing the fuel into the left wing tank to prepare for shutting down number two, I mean the right motor. He stared back blankly, then nodded. I understood what he was thinking because it wasn't something we did every day—shut down an engine in flight. We had not discussed—the normal thing to do with something that critical—transferring fuel between tanks, either.

"Okay," Kurt said. "We're 1700 pounds down—a little more than expected."

I glanced at him. "Okay."

Mark A. Putch

"If we shut down number two for thirty-seven minutes, we'll land with 800 pounds." He looked at me for a decision.

"What do you think?" I asked.

Kurt recalculated his figures before answering.

"How much is 800 pounds?" Marcia asked with shrill voice.

Casually, I said, "About ten minutes' worth."

Marcia didn't respond.

"Numbers are good," Kurt said. "I don't want to go to Nandi."

"We're going for it, then," I said. "But Kurt, we've got to get a good update to the INS, and I want you to recheck your navigation planning to the island. We've got to find it the first time around…. Or else we'll be swimming."

He went back to his maps and calculator, and finally said everything checked okay.

"What if we can't get an update with the…what do you call—"

"The INS," Kurt said.

"We go to Nandi," I said, clarifying my decision.

Bridget edged into the cockpit, standing next to where Marcia sat. We showed her the islands and briefed her on the fuel situation. She seemed happy and not particularly concerned as compared to Marcia. The sleep had apparently done her some good. We all felt better—I saw it on their faces. A bit of exuberance filled the atmosphere in the cockpit.

Kurt shifted in his seat. "I need to talk to you about your aliases and the documents."

The women huddled around the small cockpit in anticipation.

"Bridget, please get me the four portfolio folders in my briefcase," Kurt said.

"What about your laptop?"

"Bring it, too."

Approaching overhead Nandi, I said to Kurt, because he had his head buried in paperwork, "Time to update the INS."

"Here we go." Kurt pressed the update button on the INS just as we were over Nandi. He read from the display, "Nine point five miles off. Okay, it's updated."

"Not bad for twelve hours," I said. Everyone seemed to hang on my words. "How's the gas?"

"Better," he said. "1600 down."

"It's a go then," I said. The cockpit erupted in jubilation, as if we had just witnessed a space shuttle launch.

After all the hugs, handshakes, high-fives, and congratulations, Bridget handed the portfolios out according to the name on the labels.

"Marcia, would you check Duff's as we go?" Kurt asked.

"Yes."

"Open the folders, and we'll go through this quickly," he said.

They opened them and paid close attention to Kurt.

"First, notice your new names. I have made each of you a primary alias and two alternate aliases. All the aliases have assumed identities from either the USA or Canada," he said, letting them contemplate their new identities for a few minutes.

Mark A. Putch

"You think Duff can pass for a cattle rancher from South Dakota?" Marcia snickered.

"A rancher from South Dakota. Ouch!" I said.

"It's perfect for him. Think about how easy it'd be to lose yourself in South Dakota," Kurt said, chuckling.

"Right," Marcia said, drawing out the word.

We all laughed loudly. I felt the laugh all the way down in my gut, and it felt good to relieve some of the tension that had built up through the night.

"Seriously, I tried to find identities that are nondescript and anonymous," Kurt explained.

"Is that why I was born in Winnipeg?" Bridget asked.

"Yes, don't you like Winnipeg?" he asked.

"You mean Winter-peg," Marcia joked.

"Exactly, Marcia," she said.

We laughed again, another gut-wrenching laxative of a laugh. I felt like I was getting back to some semblance of sanity.

"Okay, I think you get the point. Let's go through the documents. First, you have your birth certificates and passports. Next are supporting documents such as social security numbers for American citizens and social documents for Canadians. I've included immunization records, high school and college transcripts, professional qualification documents, family history, and relatives' names and addresses, etc."

"Amazing, Kurt. How did you do all this?" Marcia asked. "How'd you know I wanted to be a doctor?"

We laughed again, as if the cockpit had been infused with laughing gas. I couldn't get enough levity; it felt great.

"Duff," he said. "Duff told me."

Marcia stood up and kissed me on the cheek.

"Seriously," Kurt said. "All the information came off the Internet. Your indigenous data—as I call it—came from people who were adopted at a young age and who had their names changed to their adoptive parents' names. You have the original birth certificates and social security numbers that were changed by the adoptive or natural parents to guarantee the child and its parents their anonymity. Supporting documents are a fabrication and a hodgepodge of credentials of those who have died but were homeless, missing, or killed in war, and the like—people who sort of disappeared from the face of the earth."

"I know what you mean, Kurt" I said.

We laughed again, this time so hard my stomach muscles started to cramp up. Feelings of elation flooded into the cistern of somberness I had been feeling before with the same spiked, rock-gut intensity. It was the perfect antidote.

"This must have taken hours," Bridget said.

"At first, yes, but I've written a program called 'Anonymity' to do the referencing and cross-referencing. That's what took the time."

"Why do we have three aliases?" Marcia asked.

"In case your primary or secondary is compromised," Kurt said.

"How do we know?" asked Bridget.

"Important question. You may never know until it's too late, but I've done one thing for each of your names that might help."

"What's that?" I asked.

"I've built Web sites on the Internet using your aliases. Sounds crazy, doesn't it?" He looked at us because we all had alarmed looks on our faces. "It's not though, because the data there can't be traced to any of us, for one, and everything there is fictionalized and protected by my own encryption code. Its only purpose is to serve what I call the Flytrap. The Web sites monitor who accesses them and cross-references their electronic names through a huge database that I borrowed from the FBI, trapping the user into an electronic fingerprint identification program. It specifically tags FBI and other law enforcement agents, including their top-secret aliases, if the program finds them prowling around your site."

"Awesome, Kurt," Bridget said.

"I thought you'd like it," Kurt said, smiling. "Now, if you tag a breach of security, assume another identity immediately. Each is independent and nontraceable to the other. You can even change your identity from what I have given you here, if you run out of aliases, God forbid. Open your folder to the next page. Okay, good. That CD is 'Anonymity.' I've given each of you a copy and it's simple to use."

"You sure?" Marcia asked. "I hate computers."

"It's real easy to use, Marcia. All you have to do is answer the questions it asks. It'll prompt you for your height, age, hair color, languages spoken, geographical region, educational background, etc. Use your imagination. There are literally millions of legitimate aliases ready to be assumed. Look at Bridget, you would never know she's a blonde."

We laughed and Bridget said, "Better watch it, buster."

"Sorry, honey. I'll make it up to you. I promise."

I thought he'd really stepped in it, and apparently so did he, but she didn't seem to mind. Her earlier anger at him must have been for the lack of sleep.

"Seriously, it takes the data and builds a personal profile within a realistic scope of parameters, then it cross-references an Internet accessed database and spits out several options. It's simple, trust me."

"I've had to trust too many people in my life to give up now," Marcia said.

We laughed heartily. Tears clouded my eyes. I took one of the towels and wiped them, carefully, one at a time, giving Pacifica a wider berth. It felt so good to laugh, a cathartic cleansing of the mind's fouled residue.

"So, I need to be able to access the Internet, right?" Marcia asked.

"I need to interrupt here for a moment." I lifted my hand and looked at the INS. We were one hundred twenty past Nandi. "Drop off point in twenty miles."

Kurt looked down. "That checks."

"Right, Marcia, all you need is Internet access. The program connects to the databases automatically. All you need to do is tell it to connect," Kurt said. He told her about how to access the Internet and explained how to do it without having a server, which was better because it would be more difficult for someone to track her. He said it varied by country, but he had a detailed instruction manual with telephone numbers for most countries. "One thing to realize, Marcia, is you're not restricted to an American identity. This program accesses many countries and as third-world countries come into the computer age, you can access their vital statistics, too. Just a word of caution, though."

"What's that?"

"If you don't speak Swahili, don't become a Kenyan."

We laughed.

"Okay. I'll brush up my Persian."

We laughed louder and longer. Everything suddenly seemed all right. We were going to make it, I knew. I felt like a new man.

"I'll help you with it later," Kurt promised.

The time to spread our wings and to put the finishing touches on a grueling night had come. "Here we go, guys," I said, pulling the power back and slipping aft of the mother ship. *"Signora Americana."* We all waved, and I know everyone had to feel some sadness as we weaned ourselves from the American udders. I rolled the Gulfstream hard left as if it were a fighter jet and let the nose drop below the dawning horizon. Pacifica 1010 faded into a light-flickering black dot as our distance grew from her.

I sensed myself soaring peacefully toward freedom like a young bird making his maiden flight from the nest. Happiness descended on the cockpit and was something real that could be worn—and smelled—like a new leather jacket. I drove her down toward the sea in a steep dive. Kurt gave me navigation instructions to the island.

"Shut down number two, Kurt," I said, my eyes focused outside as we rushed to embrace the ocean.

"Roger, sir," he said as he shut down number one. Twenty seconds later the airplane went dark and silent. Number two had flamed out.

"We've lost both engines," I said.

Marcia screamed at the top of her lungs.

"Fuck," Kurt said.

I pulled pack to shallow out the descent, but all I saw through the windscreen was ocean.

"We're going to die," Marcia said repeatedly.

"Shut up, Marcia," Bridget said. "Shut the fuck up."

"Oh my God," Marcia cried.

"What happened," I said to Kurt.

"Ah…, ah…Oh fuck, I shutdown the wrong engine."

"Get a re-light on number one," I said. "Open the cross-feed. Check ignition." We were only a couple thousand feet above the ocean.

After what seemed an eternity, Kurt said, "Okay, I've got rotation." Another long delay. "Come on baby, light."

"I can't swim," Marcia wailed.

Bridget put her hand over Marcia's mouth and dragged her into the cabin. "You're not gonna need to, damn it."

More delay, the ocean ever nearer. I commanded, "Prepare for ditch—"

"EGT rise," Kurt said with victory in his voice. "Here she comes. Number one stabilized."

"Stand by on the ditching," I retracted. "Thank God."

I heard Marcia wheezing in the back and Bridget trying to calm her.

The lights came back on as the generator spun up. I pushed up the power up on number one and started a shallow climb at about five hundred feet above the sea. "Damn, that was close. What happened?"

"I shut down number one by accident."

"Shit, I should've confirmed it." I knew I was tired because my training had been to confirm—always confirm—the *correct* engine is being shut down. That's Flying 101 stuff. "But why did number two flame out?"

Kurt studied the right wing tank fuel quantity gauge. "It has a thousand pounds in it. It's not dry…hmm. It was the angle," he said suddenly.

"That's it," I said. Our descent angle had been so steep, and the fuel quantity so low, that the boost pumps had been uncovered—starving fuel to number two. "Let's start number two to make sure it's okay."

"Roger." Kurt pulled out the checklist and went through the procedures with me following along. Number two started fine. Everything checked out, verifying our prognosis of pilot error.

The women returned to the cockpit as they realized we were going to be okay.

"Let's try it again, Kurt. Shut down number *two*," I said.

He gingerly put his hand on number two. "Number *two*," he said, mimicking me.

I said, "Number two verified."

There was a long and somber moment of silence as Kurt shut down the number-two engine.

"Whew," I said. "Way too close."

"No shit," Kurt said.

Under normal circumstances—after a fiasco like that—I would not have shut down that engine again. I would have diverted, but we had no choice. We were committed to the island. Kurt checked the navigation and gave me some corrections to my heading. Words were few and far between, but eventually—when all settled down and the confidence that we would make it returned—my tension melted off like spring runoff.

As a crew, we discussed the mistake that we had made and pledged to be more careful and to look out for each other. Bridget apologized to Marcia for yelling at her. Marcia accepted and apologized for panicking. All seemed well; we were a family again.

"I'm going to lie down until we get there," Marcia said. "I'm exhausted."

"Good idea," I said.

"You've got about thirty minutes," Kurt said.

The last half-hour went quickly because the tension of making it was over. We had saved the fuel we needed and had restarted the right engine for landing. We watched the sun bubble up over the horizon and fan long strands of orange and white light—like spilled paint—across a satiny sea. I eased the Gulfstream down to just a few feet above the surface of the ocean. A thin coating of sea spray drizzled over the windscreen like a saltwater christening.

I banked and climbed ever so slightly like a whale skimming the surface, spraying waterspouts into the air, frolicsome and carefree. Kurt and Bridget sat there taking it all in. I felt like a little boy again with the approval of my parents to enjoy myself. *Let him do it, he may never get the chance (to fly) again,* is what I think Kurt and Bridget thought.

I reminisced over military flying. We would fly low and fast over the desert, banking sharply, sometimes climbing just fifty feet to avoid a car or a semi or a little knoll or a craggy outcropping. Once we pitched up to three hundred feet off the ground in a tight, voyeuristic orbit to get a better look at the antics of a nudist colony in Nevada. Suntanned bodies sauntering about (I remembered them: men in beards, women with long strands, their triangles of matching pubic hair marching around in unison) their oasis, oblivious to the noisy boys above sharply banking their jets with ominous, tiger-shark painted noses.

"Ten miles from the island," Kurt said.

I pulled the GV up to a thousand feet and into view popped the island. "There she is," I said.

Bridget stood up from the jumpseat. "It's paradise."

"Yes, paradise," I said. I gazed admiringly at the small rectangle of land—two miles wide by eight miles long—surrounded by scalloping bands of opalescent waters. The island was a beautiful lush green oasis, part of a small chain of secluded islands, cut off from and virtually unknown to the world. Contrasting starkly to the gleaming white sand of the beach was an ebony strip of asphalt—slashed from the jungle— which paralleled the strand. The gentle waves of warm Pacific water—green as emeralds—slithered their way up the sandy shores. Bright reflections of the rising sun washed across the sand with web-like rays. I took a deep breath. "Do you smell that?"

"Smells like the sea," Bridget said.

"Smells like home," Kurt said.

I lowered the landing gear and flaps and made a smooth landing on the asphalt strip, bringing the jet to a slow crawl at the end. Exiting the runway, I shut down the left engine to save what fuel remained.

"Seven hundred pounds," Kurt said.

I brushed my hand across my forehead. "That's a very scary number after thirteen-and-a-half hours of flying."

"It's enough though," Bridget said.

I felt ecstatic to be on the ground as we taxied to the only building on the field, a large steel hangar painted white. I stopped the jet—face to face—with the tall sliding doors. Kurt got out of the airplane and slid the doors open. I taxied the airplane into the hangar and shut down the other engine. It went dark inside the jet because I didn't start the auxiliary power unit as we were short on fuel. Kurt closed the doors, making the hangar dark except for what light leaked through a window on the far side. I sat silent for a long moment. They anticipated my words.

"Welcome home," I said looking back. Jubilation, once again erupted—but briefly, for there was much yet to do.

Marcia helped me out of the seat. It was difficult to stand up for about a half-hour. It felt like walking for the first time after a month in a hospital bed. The crew encouraged me to get some sleep. They'd handle the rest, they said. I should have but couldn't because there was too much to do, and I felt responsible for getting it done. Besides, who would let somebody else handle their share of thirty-eight million dollars?

Mark A. Putch

We sorted the money out of the U.S. government boxes and transferred it into generic boxes. Bridget made five copies of the accounting of the money that we organized into numbered boxes. That took most of the day and as the sun went down, we prepared for the night.

During the night, we transferred the money onto a boat a half-mile away using a flatbed that we pulled with a small tractor. We were all armed and ready for a fight if that were to happen, somewhat paranoid it seemed, but there was nobody around. We worked stealthily in the shadows—cast sharply by a full moon—of tall, swaying palms. We loaded all the money onto the boat along with our guns, possessions and the documents Kurt had given us. Kurt drove the boat while he explained to Marcia how to use "Anonymity" on his laptop.

In a daze I vaguely recall, Bridget and I spun a few sentences about the sea and the full moon before I crashed—sleeping hard, like a teenager—until morning. Marcia woke me. "We're an hour out," she had said. I could not seem to remember a thing from the night before. The sun shone on my face through a porthole. I was still tired but feeling better.

Kurt briefed us on what to do if there were problems, but everything went fine—as if bringing in boatloads of money were everyday operations for the island nation. Everyone treated us kindly, and nobody seemed in a hurry. In port, we hired three men with a moving van to take the money to the bank, where we met the banker an hour before opening. Kurt had confirmed the arrangements of the meeting by telephone when we docked.

The banker, although brief and efficient, was cordial. His swarthy, deadpan face glowed like the northern lights when we verified his cut. We signed the papers and got the four accounts. He said it would take a month to fully fund the accounts because he had sold us his "securest investment product." We still expected a fight or something but nothing happened. It was as easy as picking daisies. The banker did not ask a single question about where the money came from. It seemed his business was to not ask questions. Somehow we knew he was trustworthy and the only doubt was in ourselves.

We went back to the boat and Kurt skippered us back to the island. I fell asleep thinking about lying on the beach with my belly anchored against the sand and the waves rocking me to sleep. I slept for an entire day, dreaming—just as Marcia said—of the future.

We stayed on the island for a week, living in the hangar and spending the afternoons on the beach. It took that long to recover from the flight (I didn't fully recover until after leaving the island). Everyone was happy that week. As a matter of fact, it had been the happiest week of my life. Island time agreed with me. All was well—until the last night when Marcia got edgy. I figured she had island fever or had thought about things too much.

An air of anticipation loomed like the isolation around us. A storm brewed. I felt the pressure dropping in my ears and smelled salt and rain in the air. It had been understood—but not discussed—that Kurt and Bridget would be leaving soon. Everything seemed apocalyptic with the storm approaching and knowing that very soon my best friend would be gone.

I went to bed on the seventh night after a party in which we all got drunk while the wind thrashed the palms against the metal walls of the hangar and whistled its spiraling trills around us. The strong pitter-patter of rain striking the metal roof continued into the wee hours. The crash of waves pounding the beach roared until after daybreak, but somehow I slept through it, waking gradually and restlessly to midmorning swelter and sunshine chasing the storm. Drowsy and heavy in the bed I twisted and turned—in and out—for another hour.

"Yes, I was like a zombie for a week: snorkeling, playing volleyball, collecting shells; yes, that's correct.

I can't tell you where. I said that a dozen times already. No. No. Yes, we did."

"Fine," the first man said. "Where did the other $38 million go?"

I stared back, expressionless.

"You stole $76 million," he peppered. "Where's the other half?"

I delayed my answer as they glared at me with unflinching eyes. "McClusky's cut," I said, as if they ought to have known.

The men seemed satisfied—victorious—as if they had everything they needed.

"Okay, is that all?" the first man asked.

"Yes. I can't remember anything else."

"Good. Here it is," the second man said.

A brown-suited man with brown polished shoes and a Franklin Graham hairstyle brought the form in and handed it to the first man. He sat down next to me, silent and reserved—poker-faced.

The first man looked at it. "Sign above your name, please." He handed it to me. I took the form, read it, then signed it underneath the words: "I, Warren Duff Hartman, do solemnly swear these statements of confession contained herein are the whole truth and nothing but the truth, so help me God." I gave it back to him.

He signed the first witness block with "Winthrop W. Tuxford Jr., Director FBI Western District."

The second and third witnesses signed the form and as the third man signed, he placed it on the table and slid it toward the first man. I pushed it along to him and a tear fell from my eye onto the paper, leaving a round water stain and smudging the type that it covered like runny eyeliner.

The men stood up as the first man placed the form with the other papers. The first man said, "Thank you, but let me ask you one more question."

"Okay."

"Why do you feel guilty now after all this time?"

I thought about it for a few seconds and gave my first honest answer in years: "I've never been caught before."

The third man ushered me out the rear door.

I awoke from the dream, feeling as if I had walked out of a hot desert mirage. My head jolted off the pillow with my hand swatting feebly at a fly circling my face. It buzzed away, alighting on a dirty sock. I lay back down—dizzy, hungover, bathed in a cold sweat—sorting reality from illusion. My body felt hollow with loneliness. After awhile—when I didn't think my head would hurt from moving it, I looked across the room to the chair with my clothes draped over it. Getting up to dress, I saw my passport with a letter tucked in it lying on the chair. Sitting back down on the bed, I read:

"Dear Duff,

The attraction I have for you is stronger than any attraction I've had for a man in all of my life. You and I fit together like tight gloves. However, under the circumstances of recent events and after much thought, I know I can't spend the rest of my life with you. In a different life I could have been the happiest woman on the planet, living with you, growing old in your arms, comforted, cherished, respected, loved, an evolving intimacy. This is the best way though, rather than putting myself through the agony of gradual distance and loss.

I'm going to spend some time with Bridget and Kurt until I find the little cottage on the beach where I'll count my days by the sunsets and the weeps, for your loss will fill a mighty sea. My gift is your freedom—the freedom you've searched for all of your days. It's yours now. I know you'll eventually understand my decision, and I hope you'll forgive me. I'll miss you, Duff, and all it could have been.

With all of my love,

Marcia"

My heart sank to the bottom of the sea as I read it over and over again, scouring the hangar and the island for Marcia, hoping desperately to awaken from the nightmare, but I never did. Mournful, I left the island on the weekly ferry to the main island where I boarded a cruise ship—attendants fumbling apologetically through my passport—that would deposit me onto the shores of another faraway land.

ABOUT THE AUTHOR

Mark A. Putch was born in Shreveport, La. He earned his wings in the U.S. Air Force and currently pilots airliners for a major U.S. carrier. Mark spends his downtime with his head in the clouds—writing.

Printed in the United States
715100006B